"I'd suggest we go get a cup of coffee, but if I'm seen consorting with you, that might cause a problem."

"I'll bet it would," she agreed. Weirdly, she felt an unfamiliar buzz of excitement. He was unnervingly good-looking; how could she not admire his broad shoulders and long, muscular body?

"I'll let you get back to work." [...] to his feet. He was so big that she fel[...] cramp of fear until she rememb[...] he'd crouched in front o[...] her in his coat, shield[...]

Expressio[...] d last time we talked, I en[...] tious, Ms. Adams."

He took a bus[...] of a pocket and tossed it on top of her [...] ven though he'd already given her one as [...] as his phone number. "In case you tore the first one up," he said, his lips twitching. "Call me if anything makes you nervous."

CRIME SCENE CONNECTION

USA TODAY Bestselling Author

JANICE KAY JOHNSON

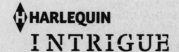

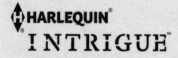

ISBN-13: 978-1-335-58263-8

Recycling programs
for this product may
not exist in your area.

Crime Scene Connection

Copyright © 2023 by Janice Kay Johnson

This is a work of fiction. Names, characters, places and incidents
are either the product of the author's imagination or are used fictitiously.
Any resemblance to actual persons, living or dead, businesses,
companies, events or locales is entirely coincidental.

For questions and comments about the quality of this book,
please contact us at CustomerService@Harlequin.com.

Harlequin Enterprises ULC
22 Adelaide St. West, 41st Floor
Toronto, Ontario M5H 4E3, Canada
www.Harlequin.com

Printed in U.S.A.

An author of more than ninety books for children and adults with more than seventy-five for Harlequin, **Janice Kay Johnson** writes about love and family and pens books of gripping romantic suspense. A *USA TODAY* bestselling author and an eight-time finalist for the Romance Writers of America RITA® Award, she won a RITA® Award in 2008. A former librarian, Janice raised two daughters in a small town north of Seattle, Washington.

Books by Janice Kay Johnson

Harlequin Intrigue

Visit the Author Profile page at Harlequin.com.

CAST OF CHARACTERS

Alexa Adams—An investigative journalist, she's used to making enemies. Her quest to expose corrupt cops has her facing armed and dangerous men. Usually fearless, she learns to be afraid—but also, maybe, to trust a man as she never has before.

Matthew Reinert—A police lieutenant, he's angry about the dirty cops in the department and steps up to confront the problem when one nasty "trick" after another is played on Alexa, who is too dedicated to back off. He won't let her stand alone and begins to suspect that may be a lifelong decision.

Art Dwyer—A detective and good friend of Matthew's, Art is investigating a series of murders. The trail seems to lead to the same cops in their department Alexa suspects. Will Art be silenced?

Alan Sharpe—This cop already *has* been silenced after trying to draw attention to conduct unbefitting an officer.

Brian Danner—A patrol officer, he resents Alexa's assault on the right of anyone wearing the badge to conduct themselves as they please.

Rick Shanahan—Another cop on the suspect list, he may be encouraging his fellow officers to skate the edge of decency for his own dark reasons.

Chapter One

Lieutenant Matthew Reinert sat behind the wheel of his department-issued SUV and frowned at an ordinary rambler halfway up the block from where he'd parked. In the past twenty minutes, the mild concern that had brought him here had morphed into alarm.

Illegal drugs were a chronic problem in his jurisdiction, just as they were in every decent-sized town in the country. Fentanyl had taken its toll, but most recently they'd been seeing overdoses from exceptionally pure, strong drugs. A new organization had moved into the northeast of Washington State, supplying meth, cocaine, oxycodone and heroin. What made these new traffickers different was the level of brutality they displayed toward competitors and used to punish dealers who had annoyed their employers. The gruesome deaths dealt as warnings weren't the norm in a city with a fairly low homicide rate.

Spokane PD had led the investigation until rumor had it that the traffickers had moved to the Spokane suburb that was Matthew's jurisdiction. Then came the tip from an occasional confidential informant, giving an address: the house Matthew was currently observing.

Matthew, as head of the major crimes division, wouldn't normally have been involved, but stories and excitement had flown. Hard *not* to hear the talk. Vice was pumped. SWAT was on the alert. Mike Kinney, deputy attorney general, had been nagging for Vice to get a move on. No doubt, he was ecstatic at what these arrests would do for his chance of promotion.

Just this morning, Matthew had been talking to the county deputy who'd led the combined city-county SWAT team. Their conversation had primarily centered on a separate joint investigation, but Brad Hargrave had complained about the pressure for him to request a warrant on the drug house.

"They aren't giving me anything!" he'd exclaimed. "And it's not my damn investigation. It's your Vice cops who should be on it."

"Not mine," Matthew had countered. "Tell you what, though. I'll see what I can find out."

Hargrave had thanked him fervently.

A quick stop by Vice detective Phil Banuelos's desk had left Matthew uneasy. Phil'd tried not to show it, but he hadn't been thrilled to see Matthew.

Phil had played the recording of the tip for him. "Guy's a low-level drug dealer," he'd said with a shrug. "Mostly reliable. He may have reason to resent this new act in town."

They'd been looking into the tip, but didn't have much yet except a couple of reports of sketchy-looking guys coming and going from the house in question, he'd admitted. "We don't really even have eyes on the house."

So how had the rumors and excitement blown up?

Impulse had brought Matthew here, detouring after another stop to look at the supposed drug house. Immediately incredulous, he'd done some online research and talked to a couple of neighbors. What he'd learned had made this mess potentially *his* business after all.

It was true that in your typical American city, drug traffickers didn't hole up in walled compounds. They hid in plain sight. He couldn't deny that this was the right kind of neighborhood, one that had slid downhill for years until recent signs of recovery. It still consisted mostly of rentals and a few vacant houses; from police reports, he knew it to be a hotbed of petty crime and domestic violence. Plenty of neighbors wouldn't complain even if they guessed traffickers did their business right next door.

That said…this particular house had been newly painted. The lawn had been mowed in the past day or two. There was a flower bed in front of the porch, for God's sake! Riotous flowering baskets hung from brackets to each side of the garage and from the beam supporting the roof of that front porch.

Matthew had yet to meet anyone even peripherally involved in the drug trade who hung flower baskets, far less fertilized them on a regular schedule.

He'd knocked on a few doors, even though he'd known he was stepping on toes. At this point, he didn't care.

The couple next door had looked astonished at his questions and insisted they hadn't seen any man there. Another less voluble neighbor across the street had appeared annoyed at being bothered but said, "She works for the newspaper. That's what someone told me."

Uh-huh.

Phil had said he'd been told it was "unclear" who owned the house, which had been a long-time rental. It hadn't taken Matthew more than a few minutes to learn that the house had sold a year ago to Alexa B. Adams, who held a mortgage on it from a local bank. There was no justification for confusion.

And Matthew knew that name.

Alexa Adams didn't just "work" for the *Tribune*. She was an investigative journalist, and a good one. A pit bull. Matthew had seen her byline in the newspaper often enough. Worse, he'd heard her name spat in disgust and even hate around the police station these past couple of months. Ms. Adams hadn't made any friends within the law enforcement community when she'd set out to identify problem officers, city and county, and to ask hard questions on why they hadn't been held accountable for questionable activities and outright breaking the law.

Wanting to believe this whole thing would die a natural death without him having to stick his nose in, Matthew decided he'd seen enough. He changed his mind when a car came around the corner and started in his direction. The sedan turned into the driveway of Ms. Adams's house. The driver parked and hopped out.

He lifted binoculars and watched as she took what was probably a laptop and file case out of her car and started for the porch, pausing to bend over and pick up the rubber-banded newspaper he'd seen being tossed onto her driveway earlier. Up to the porch and an instant later she disappeared inside. Presumably, she meant to go out again this afternoon or evening.

Lowering the binoculars, he rolled his shoulders to release tension. She was younger-looking than he'd expected, slight of build, and pretty, all of which was irrelevant. What she did took brains, determination and the kind of empathy that convinced reluctant people to open up to her. Not muscle.

And more power to her.

Knowing he needed to get back to the station and start figuring out who was responsible for stirring the pot, he still didn't reach for the ignition. He gave himself a minute to brood.

Given who the homeowner was and how deep the dislike for her went among a certain segment of police officers, he had to assume this whole thing had been aimed straight at the journalist, the goal to humiliate and frighten her. Even get her killed if the operation went south. Or maybe the instigator had never believed the raid would actually happen, just hoped word would reach her. The threat wasn't subtle.

If this fiasco turned out to have anything to do with that department-wide anger, those ruffled by her investigation could quit worrying about her and worry about *him* instead. Heads would roll. He should hand this to Internal Affairs, but he wasn't impressed with how easy they'd been on officers who *had* committed an offense. If an assault—even one disguised as an "oh oops SWAT raid"—was made on Ms. Adams, then he'd feel free to act, up to and including cuffing and charging members of his own department.

He had to ask himself how many officers had been involved in this setup. He'd absolve DA Kinney of any active role; ambition was Kinney's problem. But everyone else, including Vice detective Phil Banuelos who'd taken the tip and opened the investigation, had to be considered suspect.

Matthew grunted and started the engine.

Maybe he should leave Ms. Adams an anonymous tip, he thought with dark humor, but knew he couldn't.

UNEASINESS CRAWLED UP Alexa's spine as she slowed in approach to the park where she had promised to meet a man who'd called out of the blue. He'd claimed to be a confidential informant for the police department.

"I've given them some good tips," he'd said in a gravelly voice that made her think he was a long-time smoker. "Thing is, I seen some of 'em doing shi—I mean stuff I don't like. There're cops who take what they want from girls who work the streets, if you know what I mean. That don't seem right to me."

It didn't seem right to Alexa, either. What's more, what he was apparently willing to talk about fit right in with her investigation of dirty cops right here in this small city.

The agreed meet was to happen at this downtown park that took up only a block but had a rose garden she admired, paths and some old maple and even cedar trees. Picnic tables were tucked in here and there, along with wrought-iron benches. Two sides were bounded by streets especially busy in the evenings since this was where bars, nightclubs and restaurants thrived.

Leaving home, she'd felt comfortable about the location, even with the approach of dusk. She couldn't be the investigator she was without taking calculated risks, which included sitting down with strangers who called because they'd read her articles and columns and decided to trust her with information. Plenty of them, from drug dealers to cops, didn't want to risk being seen with her.

Now, the streetlights starting to hum into life, Alexa was bothered to realize that the park itself looked awfully dark. She backed into a spot at the curb, got out and eyed the deeper darkness lurking between those big trees and behind dense rhododendron shrubs. For the first time, she wondered how many drug deals went down in the park, and especially how safe it was for a woman to stroll one of these paths at night.

Huh. Maybe tomorrow she'd do some research and find out.

People crowded the sidewalk on the opposite side of the street, enjoying the nightlife, greeting friends, going in and coming out of clubs and restaurants.

Alexa eyed a couple of women, wearing especially skimpy attire, who stood at the far corner calling out to passing cars. Those almost had to be some of the "girls" her tipster had been talking about.

Her head turned. On this side of the street, what looked like a couple of older men sat in deep conversation on a bench at a bus stop. Otherwise…she was alone.

He'd promised, "I'll find you."

Well, she wasn't about to wander down one of those paths looking for him. *Circle the park*, she decided. *Stay on the sidewalk*. It was one block, that's all. *Keep an eye out*.

Her shoulders stiff, nerves prickling at the back of her neck, she started walking. Three-quarters of a block north, turn the corner. A couple who looked as if they'd had a few too many drinks was getting into a shiny, jacked-up pickup. They didn't even notice her. One restaurant halfway down the block was open, but otherwise traffic on this cross street had become close to nonexistent. Maybe she didn't want to circle the backside of the park. She'd just turn around when she got to the corner—

A vehicle door opened right behind her. She didn't have time to turn before a hand slapped over her face and a beefy arm wrapped around her middle. Alexa fought, kicking hard enough that her assailant swore and had to twist. He carried her only a couple of feet before slamming her down into the bed of a pickup. Her cheekbone hurt where it skidded on cold, ridged metal. The guy who'd grabbed her must have jumped up with her, because he drilled a painful amount of weight into her back with his knee.

Even as she tried to sink her teeth into a fleshy part of his hand, a bounce told her someone else had leaped into the truck bed with them. Two of them. Oh God, they were kidnapping her.

A voice said, "Do it."

Whatever hit her head *hurt* and she went limp.

ALEXA SURFACED WHEN the tailgate clanged. Hands dragged her out. Alexa grabbed for purchase with her fingers and found none. She couldn't scream; tape covered her mouth. Hands groped and ripped at her clothing.

They were stripping her, she realized in new panic. She saw her chinos fly upward.

Only a strangled sound escaped her before once again a big hand clamped over her face-. Her brief glimpse had revealed…not a face, no, only glittering eyes looking through holes in a fleece mask. He wore all black.

"Scrawny thing," one of them muttered. "Couldn't tell from—"

From? The photo above her column and on the website? If so, this wasn't random.

Somehow she freed an arm and got a handful of what felt like a windbreaker. *He* said a vicious word and tried to break her hold, twisting away. Black T-shirt beneath the windbreaker, Alexa saw that. Something fell out of his pocket and hit what had to be pavement with a tinny sound. One of the men back-handed her for her trouble and she fell to her knees. Just before that gloved hand snatched up the dropped object, she saw it from a watering eye. She *knew* that shape. It was a Wilden City PD officer's badge.

She kept fighting. Giving up wasn't in her nature. If they were determined to rape her, she probably couldn't stop them, but she wouldn't make it easy. She writhed, tried to scramble away, but got nowhere. Next thing she knew, she was facedown on asphalt as they tied her hands behind her back then her kicking feet at the ankles.

"Here," she heard one of them growl, but couldn't tell what was happening until one of the men bent over her.

"Think about what could have happened. This is your only warning," he snarled. "Back off, or you'll be sorry."

She hunched away from him, tried to stand but got only as far as her knees before she heard the powerful engine of the pickup rev to life and the crunch of gravel.

If not for the tape covering her mouth, her teeth might have been chattering.

Alexa found herself alone in darkness complete enough her eyes hadn't adjusted. When she tried to stand, she discovered she'd been tied to something. Her neck hurt so much, turning her head was hard, but she dimly saw a familiar shape. Her nose confirmed her guess. It was a dumpster. The men had left her in an alley, tied out like bait for a predator.

She blinked until she became aware of indistinct

light coming from the end of the alley she could see. A couple of dim bulbs at what were probably back doors into businesses let her view the pale gleam of her own body.

Something primal rose in her until she realized she still wore a bra and panties. A sob trapped in her throat.

If she'd been able to scream, would anyone hear and come? Did she *want* anyone to come and see her like this?

She began frantically wrenching at the cords biting into her wrists.

MATTHEW HAD JUST backed out of the parking space behind the steak house where he'd met his brother for dinner when his phone rang.

"Lieutenant?" a terse male voice said. "This is Officer Gregory. There's something you need to see."

What he needed to see, apparently, was a nearly nude woman, tied in an alley, with a piece of paper pinned to her bra that said, *Lieutenant Reinert, you should have been smart and stayed out of it.*

What in *hell*?

His mood wasn't fabulous after a day spent fruitlessly pursuing any lead at all to explain the push for a SWAT raid on Alexa Adams's house, eating up time he could ill afford from the rest of his job. Now, glad his brother had driven himself and had already left for home, Matthew rocketed out of the small lot and exceeded speed limits the five blocks to downtown. He saw lights flashing behind the busiest strip for nightlife the city of Wilden could boast. A quick jog and he turned into the alley, braking hard behind a squad car and jumping out. Another unit had responded, as well, having turned in from the other end of the alley so that it was completely blocked.

He was almost past the nearest squad car when he saw, pinned in two sets of headlights, a crouched woman, wearing only skimpy panties and bra, holding herself in a tight ball, her head lifted, her eyes both defiant and terrified.

He recognized her right away. This was the same woman who fertilized the hanging baskets and the flower bed in front of the porch of her home to coax those brilliant blooms to life.

A snicker from one of two uniformed officers, seemingly doing nothing but watching from near the front bumper of their car, had him stopping and turning. "Who was that?" he snapped.

"Ah…" He recognized them, took in the names on their chests. "You're laughing at a woman who has been brutalized?"

"They didn't tell you who she is?" one of them—Spiers—said. "It's that Adams woman. What goes around comes around."

"I'll be writing you up," Matthew said coldly before jogging the last few feet.

He took in the clothesline tied to a bar on the dumpster, one end cut, and noted pieces of more cut clothesline lying on the pavement. Seeing the inflamed strip of skin across her face where tape must have been ripped off, he swallowed his curses as he shrugged out of his leather bomber jacket and crouched in front of Alexa Adams. Why hadn't somebody already covered her?

He winced at her bruised, bloody wrists, not surprised that she'd fought to free herself.

"Let's get this on you," he said gently, wrapping the jacket around her. When her glassy gaze almost focused on him, he guided a hand into the arm of the sheepskin-lined coat then, a moment later, the second one.

He pretended to himself that he wasn't seeing her slender, even delicate, body, almost completely bared. Fury rose in him as he took in the swelling and discoloration already evident on her face. One eye was barely a slit. Had she been raped?

He called, "Do we have medics en route?"

"Can't be more than a minute away," said the officer holding a box cutter he'd just used to cut her free. Gregory, who'd called Matthew. His tone, at least, was calm and professional. "My partner is bringing something to cover her up."

Should have done that first, in Matthew's opinion, especially given the audience.

Chapter Two

Even as Matthew started to tug the zipper upward, his gaze caught on typed print on a torn sheet of white paper. Pinned to a bra as delicate as the subtle curves beneath.

Gregory'd had it word for word.

Lieutenant Reinert, you should have been smart and stayed out of it.

Had someone really believed that SWAT would swallow the tasty bait without questioning it? If so, that someone blamed him for ruining the plan. They'd found another way to scare Ms. Adams. Strip her of her dignity.

He zipped the bomber jacket closed right over the note. Less chance of messing up prints if they removed it at the hospital—although he knew quite well there wouldn't be any.

Aware another officer clutching a space blanket had come to a stop a few feet behind her, Matthew stayed where he was, crouched in front of Ms. Adams.

"I'm Lieutenant Matthew Reinert. I head our major crimes division. Can you tell me what happened?"

"I…" She tried to blink. A tear leaked from one eye. "Supposed to meet someone. Grabbed. Drove me here. Took off my clothes. Tied me up."

"Were you raped?" he asked bluntly.

She swallowed. "No."

That was a miracle, since she'd been left seminaked and trussed like a goose ready to go in the oven. Any kind of scum could have come upon her, and she wouldn't even have been able to scream.

"Who found you?" he asked.

She'd let her gaze drop, but now lifted it to his face again. "Nobody," she whispered. "There were two of them. One must have called 9-1-1. The siren and flashing lights and those headlights. Practically right away."

Matthew couldn't remember ever being angrier. Still, he fought to keep his voice gentle. "They took your clothes?"

"I think they might be in the dumpster."

Those sons of— It was all he could do not to say it out loud.

An ambulance was now backing into the alley.

"We need to take you to the hospital."

She grabbed his arm and started to stand. "Don't want to go. Not hurt that bad."

With firm hands, he settled her back on her butt. "You have to be checked out. You probably have a concussion. I'll bet your vision is blurry. There's a lot of swelling on your face."

"Ice—"

"Is in your near future," he agreed, "starting at the ER. This isn't negotiable."

A laugh that sounded scathing almost reassured him. "Got to cover your asses, I suppose."

"Maybe so," he admitted. "Do you know who these men were?"

Quite a crowd stood around them now, but as far as he was concerned, the two of them were alone in a bubble.

"Police officers," she said bitterly. Now her eyes were fixed on his belt. "Carrying the same badge *you* wear."

LYING IN THE ER cubicle, Alexa was embarrassed to realize that Lieutenant Reinert had held her hand in a warm clasp until the gurney had been pushed into the back of the ambulance. Worse yet, she'd clung to him. Apparently, his kindness had gotten to her.

No, it was more than that. He had…a strong face. A face she might have considered handsome under wildly different circumstances. Cheekbones were prominent, his jaw stubborn and shadowed by dark evening stubble, his eyes blue, or maybe gray. She couldn't tell, and was well aware a sexy face meant nothing about his character. Really, she'd been evaluating him in the hope of visible proof that he was trustworthy, because right at that moment she'd needed him.

He'd been grim, too, though. He'd said he would

see her at the hospital, but had stayed behind when the ambulance pulled out.

It took time for a doctor to exam her, order a CT scan, decide she didn't need X-rays, and turn her over to a nurse to have her multiple abrasions cleaned. Yes, once the scan was done, she got to hold ice bags to some of the sorest places.

In the midst of all that, Alexa remembered that her phone and car keys had been in the pocket of her chinos. Would someone have retrieved her clothes, however disgusting they were? Think to bring them to her?

All she wanted was to go home, climb into bed and pull the covers over her head. She'd have a chance to quit shaking, to recover her inner, hard-assed self. The one that did battle every day with the forces of cowardice and bureaucracy determined to keep her from getting her hands on the records of the two dozen law enforcement officers she was hunting as if they were foxes and she wore a red coat.

Come morning, her temper would replace this sense of humiliation, even shame, the fear because she'd been so vulnerable. Then she'd make them all sorry. But *getting* home—

"Hey."

She turned her head to see who had slipped around the curtain, although she had no doubt from that deep, calm voice who it would be.

The lieutenant, tall and broad-shouldered, held a paper bag in his hand. His keen gaze met hers. Gray eyes, she realized. The color of sharp-edged steel.

"Your clothes," he said. "We need to hold onto them for the moment. Once you get them back, you'll want to add some bleach to the wash."

Probably, she'd made a face because he smiled crookedly. "I have your phone and keys, too. I did wipe those off. Is your car downtown?"

"Yes," she croaked. "Not that far from where I was dumped, I suspect."

"Ah." He pulled a chair up close to the narrow bed and sat down. "Do you feel well enough to tell me what happened in a little more detail?"

She'd already known that Matthew Reinert was in charge of the major crimes division in the city PD. Naturally suspicious, she'd researched him with extra care because of the authority he wielded, but she hadn't come up with so much as a hint that he was dirty or less than competent. In fact, the detectives who worked under him were clean, as far as she could tell.

"Was supposed to meet someone in the park," she said. Ugh. Her lips must be swollen, making enunciating difficult.

"Who?"

She wished she felt a little less rattled. Should she tell him? Why not? She'd been led into an ambush.

"He said his name is Jim Berkey."

Lieutenant Reinert's expression changed. He knew that name and didn't like hearing it in this context— but she knew he wouldn't tell her what he was thinking. Why would he when he was a cop, too?

After all, most cops were prepared to defend their colleagues to the death, whatever their personal integrity and sense of honor.

DAMN. MATTHEW COULDN'T possibly tell her about Berkey's original tip and the cascade of consequences that, thankfully, had been cut off. If he did, he'd be fired, no question. The time might come, but not yet. If he lost his job, she'd lose her protector, whether she saw him that way or not.

"Did you record the conversation?" he asked.

Her eyes narrowed. "That name means something to you."

"It does. I think I'd recognize his voice if this really was him. If so, we might be able to put our hands on him."

She thought that over but finally nodded. "I can let you hear it."

"Good. I'm told you aren't being admitted. The nurse I spoke to is going to rustle up a set of scrubs for you to wear home. I'll take you, unless you've already called a friend or family member to pick you up."

"No." She looked away again. "I...hadn't gotten so far as thinking about how I'd get home. I didn't even know if you'd find my keys and phone. What I'd appreciate is a ride to my car."

He frowned. "Didn't the doctor suggest you might have a concussion?"

She didn't want to answer. Her expression became mulish.

"Here's the deal. I'll drive you home. If you don't have someone you'd rather call, I'll take you back to pick up your car in the morning."

"Now that I have my phone, I can call someone right now—"

Matthew shook his head. "I'd have followed you home no matter what. I want to hear the recording as soon as possible, and do a security check on your house. This attack was very personal. We need to evaluate how safe you are at home."

Seeing the appalled look on her face, he was almost sorry he'd said that—but he couldn't leave her with any illusions. Apparently, she lived alone. That made her vulnerable. Maybe nothing more would happen—but if her reputation was accurate, this woman wasn't going to heed the warning. If she went on the attack again, as he fully expected, her enemies would up the ante.

"Yes. Okay," she said after a minute. "Thank you."

The nurse popped her head in just then and handed over what she cheerfully described as the latest style in scrubs. He kind of doubted the faded blue pants and top qualified, but Ms. Adams accepted them gratefully. The nurse added a pair of rubber flip-flops that she said were from the lost and found box, no need to return them.

Matthew stepped out to let Alexa get dressed. Once she was ready, he carried the bag with her clothes, letting her clutch her phone and keys. She looked kind of cute in the scrubs, but wouldn't want to hear that from him. The flip-flops were too big and slapped loudly with every step, but she seemed to be steady on her feet.

Fortunately, the walk was short, since he'd parked in one of the slots right outside the ER entrance saved for law enforcement. That she let him help her into the passenger seat of his SUV mildly surprised him. Her cheeks might have flushed under the bright lighting, but he suspected that was from frustration and anger rather than any shyness.

"My handbag is in my car," she said suddenly, just as he fired up the engine.

"We can swing by and grab it." If her assailants hadn't already done that. If so—he hoped she didn't carry a spare house key in her bag.

She directed him to her car, which he recognized from yesterday, and gave him her keys. The cloth bag was on the floor, not quite hidden but not obviously in sight, either. He checked both visors and found what had to be the remote to open her garage door, and took that, too. He locked the door again and took her bag to his SUV.

With the overhead light still on, she immediately spotted the remote. "Oh, thank goodness you thought of that!" She found her wallet and opened it. "Everything seems to be here."

"Extra house key?" he asked.

"I don't carry one."

Her place wasn't more than a fifteen-minute drive.

They were halfway there when she spoke up. "How do you know where you're going?"

"Looked up your address." He wasn't about to admit having done surveillance on her house yesterday. If neighbors told her a cop had been asking questions, he'd hope they didn't remember his name or describe him too accurately.

"Oh." In the flickering light of streetlamps, he saw her visibly relax.

He had to wonder why she hadn't wanted a friend with her. Did she not have a man in her life she'd trust to hold her? If so, they hadn't progressed to living together, not if the neighbors were to be believed.

Well, it wasn't as if she'd let herself cry in front of *him*. He'd seen loathing when her gaze fixed on his badge. Chances were, she wasn't ready to distinguish between an honest cop and a dirty one. They all wore that same badge, after all.

And *that* got him speculating on whether she had a personal reason for her current crusade. An ugly experience with a cop pushing the boundaries to intimidate? A relative or former boyfriend who wore a uniform and had a short temper?

He couldn't ask her tonight, that was for sure.

She had been smart enough to leave on her front porch light and a living room light that spilled out the big window. Matthew parked in her driveway, got out and circled to the passenger side just in time to catch her as she started to topple out.

"Whoa!" he exclaimed, setting her on her feet. "You don't need any more scrapes or bruises tonight."

"It's these flip-flops," she mumbled, carefully separating herself from him.

He walked her up onto the porch with one hand hovering behind her. She carried herself stiffly but didn't tell him to back off.

He hadn't paid attention yesterday, but now shook his head as she unlocked the door. "We need to replace the front door."

She turned sharply. "What?"

"Better to have solid doors."

"I thought it was pretty when I bought the house."

"It is pretty," he conceded. "It's just—" He didn't have to finish.

She sighed. "One tap and an intruder could reach the dead bolt and knob."

"Exactly."

He hesitated. "I could replace it for you tomorrow. Pick up the door at whatever store in town you say, too."

Now she stared at him, suspicion in hazel eyes streaked with some gold. "Why would you do that?"

Guilt because he *should* have issued a warning yesterday when he'd realized someone in his own damn department was out to get her? Of course, he couldn't say that, and knew there was more to this impulse anyway.

"Call it an apology, just in case you're right about your assailants being cops."

She gave serious thought to that then nodded sharply. "Fine. Thank you."

Matthew felt uncomfortable during the walk-through

of her house. It felt…intimate, probably because he was so aware of her as a woman. The worst was her bedroom, naturally.

He advised her to get bars to lay in the tracks of her windows and sliding door in back. The door to the garage was steel and, he was mildly surprised, had a dead bolt that she admitted to rarely employing.

"I mean, they'd have to get into the garage first."

The side door into the garage was wood, but not in great shape. Matthew would have been able to splinter it open with one kick.

"As long as you keep the door into the house securely locked, we can probably put off replacing this one," he said reluctantly.

He thought she was relieved. Journalists probably made even less money than cops.

When they returned to the living room, he asked to hear the conversation with Jim Berkey, the one that had obviously been a setup.

She played it for him on her phone, then replayed it twice while he frowned and listened, his head tilted.

"I've never met this Berkey, but that sounds like the one message I heard. Can you send me the recording?"

Alexa debated but couldn't come up with a good reason not to do as he asked. A crime had been committed. Lieutenant Reinert *should* be investigating. However begrudging she felt, he seemed to be taking what had happened to her seriously.

He gave her his phone number, waited until a ding told him he'd received the phone recording, then said,

"I'll pick you up in the morning and we can stop at the lumberyard on the way back."

"Can you really afford the time?" she asked doubtfully.

Matthew smiled. "I can." He hoped he could talk his brother into helping. The job would go a lot faster with two.

They set a time, she locked up behind him, and he walked to his SUV, noting those glorious flower baskets in the porch light.

THE HOT SHOWER felt fabulous, but she made it record-short, unhappy that, with the bathroom door closed, she couldn't hear anything beyond it…like breaking glass. She was painfully aware of being naked, remembering when they'd torn her clothes off and she'd feared rape. She had no doubt they'd gaped at her lying on the pavement wearing only bikini panties and a bra that was as skimpy. Her skin crawled even more at the idea of the responding police officers doing the same.

Had Matthew Reinert gaped, too?

What if those men weren't satisfied with their stunt and came back for her? Might they be mad that Lieutenant Reinert had driven her home himself?

Yes, she'd seen the note pinned to her bra. She'd waited to see if he'd volunteer an explanation for it. The grimness she'd seen on his face hadn't been all about her; some of it had had to do with the pointed message to him.

What should he have been smart enough to stay out of? Did it have anything to do with Jim Berkey?

She was exhausted and aching despite a hefty dose of ibuprofen, but decided she had to eat. Feeling exposed in the kitchen, she let down all the blinds first thing, although was then uneasily conscious she couldn't see if someone was slinking through her yard.

If she had her car, she thought she'd have driven straight to the nearest hardware store and bought the window bars the lieutenant had recommended.

Of course, they wouldn't come after her so soon, she told herself. They'd need to plan. She was probably safer tonight than she would be tomorrow night or the next or—

How comforting.

She made and gobbled a sandwich, left on her porch lights, front and back, as well as the light in the hall bathroom, and finally made her way to bed. After thinking for a minute, she grabbed a dining room chair and took it to her room, wedging it beneath the doorknob once the door was closed. Doing that was probably useless, but she felt slightly better when she actually climbed into bed, pulled the covers up…and didn't sleep.

Oh, they'd pay for this, Alexa vowed.

There'd been a recent rule change she knew damn well had been put into effect to frustrate her to the point she'd give up on her quest. Obviously, they thought they *could* make her give up. Thus tonight. Well, they'd soon find out how wrong they were.

The new rule, apparently borrowed from the cities of Seattle and Everett in western Washington, said that if the same person or organization requested multiple records, the department would only work on one of those requests at a time. That meant the month to three months she'd wait for the first tranche of information she'd asked for turned into *years* when they were all lumped together. Especially when she demanded body or squad car camera footage, the delays were already unbelievable. And given that she was focusing on multiple officers, somebody, somewhere, thought they'd managed to tie up the process in knots she'd never untangle.

They were wrong about that, too, but—

Wait.

She rolled onto her back and looked up at the ceiling.

The city would expect her to sue. When she did, it would be a gimme. No, she couldn't prove she'd seen that badge, but the note addressed to Reinert had been a big mistake on their part. The threats they'd whispered to her made it clear it had been a targeted hit on a journalist who was investigating the police department. Oh yes, the you-know-what would hit the fan.

That meant she had them over a barrel.

What if she held the possibility of a lawsuit over the city and police department as a ruthless bargaining tool to compel them to hand over the records she'd requested? *All* the records? Now.

Oh yeah.

For the first time since those hands had grabbed

her, Alexa felt herself…well, not relax, she never did that, but her tension transformed into energy with a purpose.

Alexa sat up in bed, turned on the lamp and looked around for her laptop. Her mind was working too feverishly for there to be any chance of sleep, so she'd make notes. Lay out her campaign now that she had a serious weapon in her hands.

She'd do some online research on local attorneys who might be willing to take on such a formidable opponent. Then, attorney at her side, she could lay her cards on the table.

They were all going to be deeply sorry when they realized they'd dealt her four aces.

Chapter Three

After she'd researched attorneys and had secured a midafternoon appointment with the one who struck her as the best bet, Alexa got dressed in expectation of Matthew's arrival. No, Lieutenant Reinert's. He had his own agenda. They weren't friends. She felt sure he wouldn't like her asking about the note that chided him for an unknown offense that clearly involved *her*.

When she heard his truck in the driveway, she hurried out, almost immediately shivering. March in eastern Washington was more winter than spring. She wouldn't be outside long enough to bother going back for a coat, though.

The guy who lived on one side of her seemed to spend an awful lot of time doing something to the engine of an old car sitting on cinder blocks instead of wheels. Today, a group of his buddies hung over the engine with him, beer cans in hand despite the early hour. A couple of them nodded when they eyed her. That was about as friendly as this neighborhood got.

On the other hand, she wasn't the most popular

woman in town, so maybe she was the lone pariah on the block.

The lieutenant got out to greet her, but another man sat in the back seat of the extended cab pickup. Alexa decided her dismay was because the presence of someone else might keep her from confronting Reinert about what he knew.

But, damn it, if she got the labor to install a new door out of this, she wouldn't complain.

"Morning," the lieutenant said in that distinctive voice. "I brought my brother along."

Today he wore khaki cargo pants and a long-sleeved black T-shirt. He was missing only the badge and holstered gun at his belt, which were probably locked in the glove compartment.

"Dragged his brother along," the much younger guy in the back called out.

Alexa laughed, hearing how cheerful he sounded.

"Meet Nate," the older brother said with good humor, opening Alexa's door for her.

She climbed up into the cab, remembering how he'd boosted her last night in the hospital parking lot. His hand had been right on her butt, if she was remembering right.

Putting on the seat belt, she swiveled to see Nate. The resemblance between the two men was obvious, from the strong bone structure to the gray eyes, although Nate was thinner, less…finished. And there had to be a big gap in age between the brothers—at least ten years, and likely more.

"Yeah, I was an oops baby," Nate supplied, likely

having read her expression. He sounded undisturbed by what might be fact or might be supposition, but she had to wonder.

"Oh," was her intelligent response.

The affection between the brothers was obvious as they maintained an easy banter during the drive downtown, where the lieutenant was able to pull up right behind her car.

"Hasn't been stripped," he observed.

"In Wilden?"

He grinned. "You never know."

Nate hopped out to join his brother in the front seat as she unlocked her own car and said, "Home Depot seems to have the best selection in doors, if that's okay."

"We'll be right behind you."

Her car started fine, although she found it unnerving if also comforting to have a huge black pickup hugging her bumper all the way across town.

They parked next to each other and walked in together. Matthew broke off to collect the locking devices for her windows and patio door. He hadn't actually pulled out a measuring tape last night, but claimed to have a good idea of dimensions. She and his brother headed for the area where doors were displayed, Alexa very conscious of the sidelong looks her bruised face attracted.

"I suppose any glass is verboten," Nate remarked as she gazed wistfully at a gorgeous, solid walnut door with beautiful inset beveled glass.

"I'm afraid so." Oh, well—she couldn't afford the price anyway.

"He's big on security."

She glanced sideways. "Always?"

"Pretty much."

"I suppose that makes sense, given what he must see every day."

Nate grinned at her. "So I tell myself."

"I hope you didn't have anything important planned today."

"Nah. He has an old place he's working on. I'm his apprentice. We usually have a good time."

This felt awkward. "I don't know why he's doing this, but you really don't have to. So…thank you."

He gave her an odd look but said only, "No problem. Hey, what about this one?"

The door was solid wood rather than steel, but had beautiful detailing on the panels and was stained a rich cherry color she liked. When Matthew reappeared, he conceded that it would do. "It could be broken in, but—"

She rolled her eyes. "Why would anyone bother when they could just tap a windowpane?"

His grin reminded her of his brother's, but her reaction was quite different. It was as if her heart did a somersault. Alarmed, she thought, *Oh no. He's conning you. You* know *he is.* She absolutely couldn't afford to become susceptible to his smiles or gritty voice or powerful shoulders.

She paid and then drove home while the two men collected the door at the back of the hardware store and followed. There, they unloaded the door, the new hardware she'd also picked out, and tools. After hovering for a minute, she decided she couldn't do a single thing to help and was just in the way. She'd pretend they were hired workmen. Be as impersonal as possible.

Sitting at her dining room table, she checked messages on her laptop and phone, responded to a few emails, and pretended she didn't hear the crack of wood giving way, the thud of a hammer, the thump as they presumably set the new door in place. Never mind their voices somewhere in the same register, Nate's less gritty.

And why am I staring into space?

At one point, she offered them iced tea, which both guzzled. She could offer to make them sandwiches—

No, she couldn't. None of this was Nate Reinert's fault, and it *was* nice of him to help, but she had no reason to be more than pleasant to a law enforcement officer high in the hierarchy of the department she was investigating. The department that was fighting back, tooth and nail, to keep her from learning anything about officers who should have been long since fired or never hired. She had trouble believing Lieutenant Reinert didn't know about the history of some of those officers.

When he appeared in the kitchen to hand her the keys to her new door, she hopped to her feet, as if that could alleviate her awareness of her average height and slender, less-than-formidable body versus his sheer size.

"I hope you know this doesn't mean I'm going to back down."

A first hint of a smile deepened a crease in his cheek. "Never crossed my mind. I've read your columns, Ms. Adams. I'm not an idiot."

"Oh. Well, then, thank you." She transferred her gaze to the younger Reinert, who'd appeared behind his brother. "Both of you."

She walked them to the door, admired it and repeated her thanks. Nate bounded down the porch steps and headed for the pickup. Matthew hesitated, giving her the chance she'd been waiting for.

"I need to know what that note meant." That came out more belligerently than she'd intended. "You already knew something before I was kidnapped."

His hesitation went on long enough to heat her temper, but she managed to keep her mouth shut until he said, "Can this be off the record?"

"No!"

"Then I'm afraid at this point I can't tell you what I suspect motivated the message to me, except to say that you've stirred up some serious anger within the department."

"As if I didn't know that. What I didn't expect was a physical attack."

"I didn't, either. I was thinking it would be more along the lines of a dead rat on your doorstep." His shoulders moved. "A warning. If I'd guessed—" He shook his head. "I promise you that I'll do my best to find out who attacked you. This was completely unacceptable."

"While employing and promoting officers who provide cover for drug dealers, bully prostitutes and rough up people whose only crime is looking different from them *is* acceptable?"

His eyes turned cold and his expression hardened. "I didn't say that, and don't believe it. I'll be putting my best detective on this." He nodded and turned away.

Alexa stepped back. Just before she closed the new door, he paused. "Watch your back, Ms. Adams. Call if you need me."

Then he walked away, and she locked the dead bolt and bent to rest her forehead against the door. She needed a moment before her knees quit quaking.

"SHE THANKED YOU. She can't be that mad," Nate said.

Scowling ahead at the jackass who'd been so determined to make a left turn, he'd brought the busy intersection to a tangled halt, Matthew only grunted in response to his kid brother's determined optimism. Nate always had been unnaturally sunny.

If Alexa Adams really appreciated his gesture, she'd forgotten it by the time she demanded answers at the end. He couldn't even blame her. She had a right to know—but Matthew knew damn well that he'd be expected to keep his mouth shut. That hadn't changed.

"How come we're just sitting here?" his brother asked. "You could blast the siren, and even give that guy a ticket."

"I'm not a patrol officer." His truck did have a siren

and flashing lights he could use in an emergency, but this didn't qualify as that.

The light changed and traffic resumed a normal flow.

"Let's grab a burger," he suggested.

"Yeah! You owe me!"

Matthew grinned, although it required an effort on his part. What happened last night didn't sit well with him. The way Alexa had shrank from him today the one time he'd passed close to her was worse.

Not "Alexa," he corrected himself. Ms. Adams.

His phone rang. Recognizing the number, he answered with a "Reinert."

"You know I've been hunting for that damn CI all morning," his sometime detective partner told him. "Far as I can tell, Berkey's done a bunk. Why would he do that if he was straight with his information or really meant to meet up with the reporter last night?"

"Because he's afraid one of the traffickers would have guessed where the tip came from? Because he set her up *a second time*?"

Art Dwyer growled something wordless.

"Oh, by the way, I'll be sending you the recording from Ms. Adams. I'd swear it's the same voice."

"Okay. I'll keep on it. You done with your good deed?"

"I am. I was just about to feed my brother as recompense."

"You *like* construction."

Matthew couldn't deny it. In his limited spare time, he was currently restoring a 1910 house that had caught his eye even if it was three or four times too big for a single man, and he'd dragged Art in as assistant more than a few times. Nate even more often, of course.

Dwyer gusted a breath. "You taking the afternoon off?"

"I wish." He didn't hold back although Nate was eavesdropping. He could trust his brother's discretion. "Panic has been spreading. I'm to join a meeting to discuss Ms. Adams's allegations. The current hope is that we can get away with insisting she made up the details that point to cops as her assailants."

"We both know she's telling the truth. The note to you is a giveaway if nothing else."

"You and I aren't in denial." He sighed. "If there's any afternoon left when the meeting lets out, I'll work from home. Unless something comes up." He'd cast his bread on the waters and mostly could only wait until he saw who nibbled. He didn't have to be at his desk to do that.

"Something always comes up," his fellow detective said morosely before ending the call. No goodbye necessary.

"OF COURSE SHE'LL SUE!" Matthew snapped. Was the county executive really that naïve? He didn't say that but could tell from her expression that she knew what he was thinking.

A babble of voices broke out that made his eardrums quiver, and not for the first time since he'd taken a seat at the long table in the conference room to discuss the debacle. Did these people even listen to each other?

He didn't fully understand what this meeting was supposed to accomplish. Representatives from county government, city hall, both law enforcement agencies, all gathered to point fingers and try to pretend *they* had no responsibility for last night's disaster.

And no, the bad intel about the drug traffickers hadn't come from the county commissioner or city mayor. Nobody in this room had snatched a journalist, banged her up and done their best to humiliate her. What he hated was finding out that the prevailing opinion was exactly what he'd anticipated—everyone wanted to frame Alexa Adams as a liar.

Matthew wished like hell he hadn't been compelled to attend this meeting. He'd much rather get back to tracking down every single person who had any connection to Jim Berkey, or who'd done either shoddy surveillance or flat-out lied about the house Berkey had identified as belonging to the traffickers. Matthew didn't believe for a minute that it had just been an error, as he'd been told several times already this morning. Wrong address. Too bad, but that kind of thing happened.

Really? It was chance the home belonged to a reporter investigating bad cops? The same reporter who had been attacked the next day?

He wasn't impressed with the self-congratulatory tone, either.

See, the raid didn't happen.

Our precautions are solid.

So solid, nobody had made a serious attempt to determine whether the tip was valid until Hargrave had questioned it, and Matthew's curiosity had been awakened.

They all knew full well that a couple of the most notorious police shootings in the country had supposedly been the result of a wrong apartment number or address. In his opinion, there was no excuse for that kind of screwup. Ever. Or being so offhanded about an attempt to manipulate SWAT.

His gaze drifted to Mike Kinney, who wouldn't admit for a minute that his ambition had led to a push to jump the gun.

But what roused Matthew's temper the most was the repeated insistence that Ms. Adams had no proof whatsoever that she'd seen a police badge.

"Even if she saw one," the police chief snapped, "what's to say it was ours? Badges look a lot alike. It could even have been a prop if someone wanted to mislead her."

"And the threat they made?" Matthew felt compelled to ask.

"Who knows what investigations she's involved in? Even she doesn't claim it was specific. And that's if the threat was ever really made."

The undersheriff's eyes met Matthew's. A steady man in his forties with a solid career in law enforcement, he'd mostly stayed quiet so far, but now he spoke up. "The note—" a copy of which lay in front of the Wilden police chief "—certainly implicates local officers. What could it refer to besides the attempt to justify a raid on Ms. Adams's home, which was squelched by Lieutenant Reinert's research?"

People started talking over each other.

"It could mean anything!"

"Offer this woman a settlement right away," the city attorney declared.

Matthew pushed back his chair and stood, momentarily silencing the room. "Maybe before you try to pay her off, you might consider offering the respect of letting her know if the assault was committed by local officers, they'll be appropriately punished. Rushing to discredit her will do nothing but make her believe she's right that both our departments are tolerating dirty cops and that we'll go to the wall to defend them."

"She's a damned journalist!" the police chief snapped. "We admit any culpability, she'll be on us like—" Belatedly cautious, he cast a glance around.

"I think it's safe to say she won't take this lying down anyway," Matthew pointed out.

"Unless she signs a nondisclosure agreement." That was the city attorney again.

"I never knew how much of an optimist you are." Her face tightened.

Matthew shook his head. "I doubt you could come up with enough money to silence Alexa Adams. What she wants is the truth. I suggest we think about giving that to her." Even knowing he wasn't doing his career any favor, he shoved the chair back up to the table and walked out.

His job was to investigate, and that's exactly what he was going to do. That, and worry about the second strike—or was it the third?—that he fully anticipated.

Chapter Four

"They're going to fight this thing in every way possible," Alexa's new attorney told her.

Diana Troxell was maybe midforties, her sleek dark hair cut in a bob, her makeup always flawless. She had a steel magnolia reputation—a smile that was downright sweet, and a way of slicing and dicing her opponents with surgical precision. Alexa had seen her in action in court several times and admired her refusal to back down. There'd been a couple of times Alexa had had to blink and think, *Wait. Did she really just say that?*

She'd already thanked Diana for getting her in so soon. Now she queried, "They?"

Diana waved a hand. "City, county, cops. All of them."

Alexa said, "You do know they'll try to deny the two men who set up a fake meeting and jumped me were cops?"

The attorney made a couple of quick notes. "Of course they will. Too often, politicians can claim gravity has ceased to exist and make people believe them, as we both know. In this case, that's not what I meant, though. Sure, they'll claim you misunderstood the threat, but from what you've told me, *something* happened earlier that they didn't share with you. Something that could have been really bad. I expect them to tell me what that was.

"The note left with you letting Lieutenant Reinert know his intercession wasn't appreciated is the clincher for us. They won't want to have to explain whatever went on to a jury.

"What I anticipate is an offer to pay you off, preferably right this minute, before you have a chance to get greedy or think you can add an another zero or two to that number. But when you turn down the payment and demand they open the door to their records? Let you rummage around so you can publicly excoriate officers in their own police departments, thereby shaming the higher-ups for not even trying to make those same officers walk the straight-and-narrow? For hiring officers who've been fired from other departments for unethical, racist or even illegal acts?"

"You think this is hopeless."

Diana's grin had a sharklike quality she rarely displayed. "No, I'm just saying they're not going to leap at the opportunity to save themselves some money and say, 'Sure. We have nothing to hide.' Even if we achieve an agreement, I'm going to guess a lot of the records you're seeking will turn out to have been misfiled or lost. There'll be apologies, promises to find whatever it is, and time will drag by."

"No different than what I've experienced this past six months."

"Exactly. That said, once we have the right signatures on a dotted line, we'll have recourse to legal actions when they don't fulfill their agreement. I'll *enjoy* taking those legal actions." The grin widened. "So much, I'll happily take on your case pro bono. I respect what you're trying to do. Citizens should be able to trust their police officers. I was taught when I was a kid that I could. Nobody mentioned those cops that use their guns and authority to threaten people because of a personal beef or lie on their reports and in court about how a violent incident escalated, or bullied teenage girls into sexually servicing them."

"And that's just skimming the surface," Alexa agreed. "There are at least twenty complaints on file about a county deputy who clearly profiles the people he pulls over, or which side in a dispute he comes down on. And then there are the ones who have really friendly relationships with a few prostitutes. Why arrest when you can enjoy?"

The attorney leaned forward. "I do have an obligation to remind you that you're taking a hard road when you could be cashing a good-sized check instead. That said, I can hardly wait to read your articles when you blow the lid off that kettle."

"If I wanted good-sized checks, I'd have gone to law school."

The two women smiled at each other.

With a brisk nod, Diana said, "I'll call to set up a first meeting. I can hardly wait to sit down with them.

They won't have a clue what you want, or a game plan to stop you."

"We can only hope."

HITTING NOTHING BUT dead ends wherever he turned, Matthew hardly tasted a bite of the sandwich and bakery cookies he'd brought for lunch on Monday. He ate mechanically, despite a churning gut, wishing he'd felt he could have taken the day off. Any day.

He'd ignored a few calls from people he didn't really want to talk to, but had barely finished lunch when his phone rang and he saw Art Dwyer's number.

"Nothing on Berkey. A dead woman was found in a dumpster in an alley backing our favorite stretch of bars," Art said. "First responder recognized her, says she's a prostitute who worked that area. Garbage truck already did a number on the scene, but it sounds like she was killed a day or two ago. Garbage worker didn't like the smell and was smart enough to stop the mechanism before he dumped the load into his truck. He took a look."

"Those guys should have strong stomachs."

"Not strong enough."

"Were you up for this one?" Matthew asked. Dwyer had been concentrating on picking up any trace of Jim Berkey, and he was dogged on that kind of trail.

"Everyone knew I've been working the other murders of prostitutes."

Three, to date, within the past year, as well as a couple of previous ones. Yes, prostitutes were vulnerable members of the population, but Wilden wasn't a big enough city to expect so many murders that were so similar.

"I wanted to get in on this one from the beginning," Art added. They all had their crusades.

"I'm sorry." And he was, but Art, like him, couldn't resist dedication to the job when it kicked in.

Matthew made the drive in just over ten minutes, parking on the street. The uniform guarding the end of the alley recognized him and waved him by. He edged past the garbage truck and was hit hard by the stench. Harder than usual; he wasn't sure it was possible to become accustomed to the smell of a decomposing body, human or other mammal, but the myriad foul smells made for a horrific medley.

Art was deep in conversation with a couple of uniformed officers and two guys in dark green uniforms indicating they were probably the garbage collectors. Seeing Matthew, he grimaced in greeting, and jerked his head toward the dumpster, back on its wheels on one side of the alley.

Matthew donned latex gloves he almost always carried and hoisted himself up to look inside. He couldn't see much of the body, maybe because the contents had been stirred during the gathering process, but enough. A bare breast and shoulder, bleached-blond hair sticking to what was left of a face seen in profile, a spike-heeled black boot slimed by some unknown substance, and a swarm of black flies.

His favorite kind of crime scene.

He and Dwyer left the dumpster and its contents to the CSI duo who had pulled up to the other end of the alley. Matthew spoke briefly to the middle-aged garbage collector who'd spotted the body and then let him and his partner go on with their route. Apparently, his boss hadn't been compassionate enough to suggest they take the day off. Then the two detectives divided the businesses that backed onto this alley to canvass them.

Question number one. Why hadn't anyone tossing the past day or two's refuse into the dumpster given a thought to the stench?

Matthew was grateful that Art was there, even if he did feel guilty since poor Art had been more than due a weekend off.

Matthew's first interview was with the manager of the bar that had a back door opening ten or twelve feet from the dumpster in question.

The guy shrugged at the question. "Alley always reeks. We get some homeless sleeping there sometimes. It was bad enough yesterday, I glanced behind both dumpsters to be sure one of them hadn't died, and figured it was an animal." He sighed. "You identified the victim?"

"We think it's one of the girls who work the neighborhood. Can't be sure yet. You get to know them at all?"

"Yeah, they duck in here sometimes when the weather is especially bad. Never stay more than a short while to warm up or wait out a squall. You know they'd be in trouble if they did. I shouldn't let them, but…" He shrugged. "I don't let their pimps cross my doorstep." His voice had hardened. "Far as I'm concerned, they can sit in their damn cars. I've tried talking to girls when I can see they're kids, but—" Another shrug.

Matthew nodded. Siccing social services on teenagers who'd already swallowed the hook rarely did any good, either. He hoped this victim wasn't a kid, although he didn't deceive himself that any of them would live long, happy lives.

He was becoming something of an expert on the lifestyle, since the city had seen the string of murders of prostitutes this past year. Statistically, more than usual, although investigators hadn't been able to positively declare that one perpetrator was responsible. Matthew and Art had their suspicions, but these were some of the toughest homicide cases to solve. Getting away with killing a hooker was all too easy.

Art and he met on the sidewalk half an hour later, neither having learned anything useful. Nobody had seen a thing. Heard a thing. Most bartenders didn't remember what girls they'd seen walking the sidewalk the past few nights, or whether they'd noticed a familiar one missing.

Of course they didn't.

Maybe they were just being honest. It wasn't their business; that kind of activity wasn't any different from passing traffic except when there was a fender-bender.

"We need to come back tonight," Art grumbled. "Michelle isn't going to be happy."

Wives were rarely happy about a detective's erratic hours, but Art Dwyer's marriage was an exception to what Matthew had come to think was the rule. Art had been a cop for almost twenty years, having hit the big four-oh in July. Today, when he told her he had to go out again, his wife would scold him, kiss him and send him out with an insulated mug of hot coffee.

Occasionally, she did or said something that gave Matthew a pang of… Not jealousy, exactly. Yearning for a relationship like that? Maybe.

Strangely, Alexa Adams's face appeared before his mind's eye, and he almost smiled. Now, *there* was a tough woman who'd be so busy hunting down evil, she wouldn't think a thing of her husband doing the same, even if he carried a gun doing it and risked his life in a way she didn't.

Even the impulse to smile died as Matthew remembered last night and how easily a half-naked woman tied out like bait in an alley could have met a worse fate—one that might have left her dead.

STANDING UNDER THE streetlamp so he could see the two women's faces, Matthew scribbled in his small spiral notebook. He kept a wary eye on the sidewalk traffic, even though bar hopping was less popular on a weeknight. Still, this was a nice evening.

"Color?" he asked.

Both hookers were sure the last time they'd seen Tansy, she was getting into a pickup.

"I don't know," one said.

She was so young, he was tempted to haul her in to find out her real age and whether she had family looking for her, but knew he wouldn't tonight. He needed cooperation.

"It was dark," said the other prostitute, who looked more like she was pushing forty years old, which probably meant she was twenty-five or so. "And I didn't pay that much attention. Why would I?"

"Even at night, you'd have been able to tell if it was white," he argued. "If you can picture a pickup, you must have an idea of color."

They looked at each other.

"It wasn't white," the girl offered. "It was more, like, dark. Black. But it could've been red or blue or, I don't know, gray?"

He did know, but had hoped one of them might have seen the truck passing under a streetlight as it drove away.

"No glimpse of the driver?"

The glance at each other looked shiftier. To this point, he thought they'd told him the truth, but knew there was something they didn't want to say.

Two heads shook.

"You're sure you haven't seen her since?" he asked.

This time, the headshakes seemed straight up, even though they were getting antsy, aware their handler was nearby and irritated because they weren't working.

"Okay," he said. "Thanks. Here's my card—" he handed one to each "—in case you think of something."

They were so eager to get away, they stumbled over their own feet. Nodding, he strode off, scanning the pedestrian traffic for any other working girls.

He found a few more women to talk to, finally rejoining Art Dwyer a couple of blocks down.

Art said, "Nada. You?"

"Pickup truck. Probably not white or any other light color."

Art's snort said it all. This was eastern Washington. Any man who didn't drive a brawny pickup would have to expect to defend his masculinity in another way.

Matthew had an excuse; he owned one because he needed it to haul lumber and other supplies for the never-ending renovation of his house. If not for that, he actually would have preferred to drive something that handled better in snow and ice.

Somehow, he'd bet the ninety percent of other cops in his department who drove pickups would have their own excuses.

Looking around, Matthew said, "Call it a night. I can watch the camera footage of the alley then knock off, too." *He* didn't have anyone waiting at home for him.

"Appreciate it," Art said. They walked together until he veered off toward his truck—charcoal gray—and Matthew continued to the one and only bar that bothered with a security camera. Not one in front, unfortunately, but the owner had gotten tired of the hookups and drug deals taking place behind his business and had hung a big sign on the inside of the back door saying, You Go Out, You'll Be On Camera.

As it happened, Matthew had already watched the segment taped that he had hoped would show traffic in the time frame of the assault on Alexa. Not a single vehicle had traversed this block of the alley during that stretch of time. He hadn't been surprised, since most Wilden PD officers would know to avoid the camera.

The bar wasn't on the block where the body had been dumped, but Matthew could live in hope that, unlike local police officers, the killer didn't know about the camera and had driven several blocks down the alley rather than risk being seen turning at the corner and then into the alley where the body would be found.

Except, of course, he'd hoped it wouldn't be discovered until the garbage truck dumped its load at the transfer station—or, better yet, at all. Nobody would likely have gone to the police just to report a prostitute was missing. If they had, any action taken would have been minimal, given that it was reasonable to assume she'd simply fled her pimp and/or maybe even the lifestyle.

At the bar, Matthew was showed into an office and, allowed to close the door, he shut out the live music and voices in front while he pored over the usual grainy, black-and-white film. There was just enough action in the alley that he couldn't fast-forward as much as he'd like—an occasional car or truck moving slowly, a few drunks probably taking a shortcut to their vehicles, the easy-to-spot homeless wearing multiple layers of clothing or carrying all their possessions, one pushing a heavily laden shopping cart. Given the harsh winters, the numbers of homeless were well below what was common on the western side of the state, but there were always a few who couldn't deal even with nights in a shelter.

Nothing stood out to Matthew, but he made particular note of all pickups since he didn't yet have an approximate time of death to better pinpoint realistic possibilities. In a few cases, he could make out license plate numbers. For all he strained his eyes, sometimes he failed. One black pickup appeared to have something covering the plate. Unfortunately, that one had been traveling east-west, which meant the driver was on the far side of the vehicle. Matthew couldn't even tell if he was looking at a man or woman.

Eventually, frustrated, he thanked the bar owner, who agreed to copy three days of footage and get it to Matthew. An expert could probably enlarge details.

Then he went home, reminded too well why his investigators had yet to so much as identify a suspect in any of the murders of the prostitutes who worked the streets within a ten or twelve block area of his city. Art Dwyer in particular had been giving it his all.

Back when Matthew had been in uniform, he'd arrested enough johns during stings to develop a serious disgust for the business. Too many of the men who thought nothing of using some fourteen-year-old girl were respected businessmen, contractors, accountants, plumbers, real estate agents. Even an occasional reverend and one city councilman. As much as the murders and other crimes Matthew had seen, it was those johns, embarrassed because they'd been caught but not ashamed of their abuse of vulnerable women, who'd turned him into a cynic.

And most of all, he despised the cops who were supposed to be policing an illegal activity but instead blackmailed women with no good alternative into offering sex.

Them, he wanted to bring down.

Chapter Five

Alexa parted the blinds in the guest bedroom and watched a car passing on the street. Had it slowed down in front of her house? No, she was being paranoid. After a moment, she yanked at the window to make sure the lock was secure then went to her home office to do the same.

Beyond the reach of the light over the patio, her backyard was dark and shadowy. She'd liked the mature shrubs surrounding the house when she'd bought it, but now those deep shadows made her uneasy. She'd never see someone lurking beside that big lilac or the butterfly bush. Maybe she could cut the bushes back—

Oh, for Pete's sake. She'd never had a break-in before, not here and not at the apartments she'd rented in the years before buying the house. The attack had been committed by cops, and she'd been lured out of her home. No break-in required. As it turned out, they hadn't wanted to steal anything or rape her.

Just humiliate her, she reminded herself, stomach tightening before she shoved at the memory. Or if she didn't back off from her investigation would another assault escalate?

Go to bed.

Since she'd now checked every window and door, a few twice, just as she had last night, she'd run out of excuses. Alexa seriously thought about finding a weapon to tuck under her pillow—a butcher knife? a hammer?—but talked herself out of it again. Would she have gotten anywhere trying to fight back with that kind of weapon against two brawny men with police training? Plus, neither a hammer nor a knife was of much use when facing an opponent carrying a semiautomatic gun.

She brushed her teeth then braided her hair. The night was warm, but she wore flannel pajama pants and a baggy T-shirt instead of skimpier attire. Normally, she'd open the window to cool her room, but not tonight. Instead, she went back out to the hall to nudge up the air-conditioning.

Finally, she crawled into bed, where she lay rigid, listening to every sound, categorizing each, trying to remember if it was normal or out of the usual. An hour later, she was no closer to sleep than she'd been when she turned out the bedside light.

Surely, sleep would come.

It did, but not until well after midnight. Fortunately, she had no grand plans tomorrow. She planned to work on an article her editor was not so patiently waiting for. Unrelated to her more intense focus on dirty cops, this article was about some money the county public works department had either misplaced or misspent—it wasn't yet clear. They'd been dodging questions, and the county executive had asked for patience before the newspaper went public with something that might just be an honest mistake.

Most people came clean about honest mistakes, in Alexa's experience. Since the attack on her couldn't be called an honest mistake—and the county and city attorneys had made a lot of excuses to put off meeting with Diana—Alexa had written a colorful story about it. Her editor had strategically held it for the Tuesday morning paper—right before Diana met with the city and county powers that be.

Barely out of her shower come morning, Alexa heard her phone ringing. She expected multiple calls in response to the article and planned to give interviews rife with emotion and bewilderment for the benefit of the viewers of local TV news.

By midmorning, all those city, county and law enforcement higher-ups would see the writing on the wall. And, by God, she'd keep the pressure on as long as she needed to. Yeah, she could issue not-so-subtle threats as well as they could.

She cracked her front door, looked both ways and crept out onto her porch to snatch up her newspaper before rushing back inside and locking the dead bolt.

MATTHEW WAS DETERMINED to push for this murder to be worked as hard as every other one, even though public interest tended to be anemic when the victim was someone with a police record. Tired of being stuck behind the desk too much of the time, he was glad to take an active role in the investigation, partnering with Dwyer.

Tansy Gould's fingerprints were on record, confirming her identity. Full name: Tansy Elizabeth Gould. Age: twenty-two. Height: five foot three. Weight: one hundred and four, confirmed by the ME's office. She was currently blond, but her now-expired driver's license listed her as having brown hair and hazel eyes.

The autopsy produced no surprises. Her cause of death was straightforward: a bullet had ripped out her carotid artery. Some lucky crime scene investigators were giving that alley another once-over and digging through the dumpster in search of a bullet. Of course, nobody had heard a gunshot, which might mean the murderer had used a suppressor. But she also could have been killed elsewhere and then transported back to her own neighborhood. It did appear her body had been wrapped in a sheet of plastic that had torn as garbage was dumped on top of her and then partially twisted off when the dumpster was lifted and upended before the process was halted and reversed after the garbage collector with the sensitive nose took action.

Starting his day, Matthew read his morning newspaper while he ate a bowl of cereal. Alexa Adams hadn't held back either the details of the assault, or the fear she'd experienced. The anger was there, too, plenty powerful, as was her certainty she'd been attacked by cops fearing her investigation into their wrongdoing. To his surprise, she hadn't mentioned the note directed at him.

He left the paper on the table and grabbed his keys, anticipating another day of fingerpointing.

Matthew's first task once he reached the station was to call the victim's mother in Bellingham, on the other side of the state, to tell her not only that her daughter was dead but that she'd been murdered. He'd heard that same scream before, but never got over the painful empathy.

Mrs. Gould's story didn't surprise him. Tansy and her father had never gotten along. She'd run away several times, starting when she was thirteen, become involved in the drug scene, and finally, at seventeen years old, completely disappeared.

Weeping, Mrs. Gould said, "I tried to convince myself she'd come home someday. If she looked, she'd have seen on Facebook that her daddy died. I guess mostly I suspected someone like you would call me eventually with this kind of news."

He promised to keep her informed. He'd be in touch as soon as the body was released.

Tansy's mother was crying hard when he ended the call, feeling like he'd been kicked in the chest. Even if they made an arrest, what would that mean to a mother who not only had to live without her child, but also knew how wretched that life had been and how horrific her death?

Having already taken a few calls from other people in the department who'd read Alexa's article this morning, he was able to easily switch mental gears when his boss paused by his desk to let him know of the recriminations flying between city and county.

A lot of people who rarely showed their faces at the station were probably working today.

"Nobody will admit publicly that they believe her, but they know damn well it was cops who set up that scene. Sheriff's office insists it happened in town. Couldn't have been *their* deputies. Chief wants to find a way to dump responsibility on them. What *I* want is to find out who those two men are, and whether they're behind the tip that was supposed to mushroom into a SWAT raid."

If anybody working with Art had located Berkey, Matthew felt sure he'd have been updated. Undercover Vice detectives were supposedly looking, too, but, for all he knew they'd taken the d, ay off.

"Guy's probably running for his life," Matthew reported now in disgust, "but he'll surface. If talking will save him from a prison term, I have to believe he'll name names."

The deputy chief grimaced and nodded. "Keep on it," he said unnecessarily, rapping his knuckles on Matthew's desk and walking away.

Somebody had kindly left the morning *Tribune* smack in the middle of the blotter on his desk where he couldn't miss it. He read it again, and noted that the murder of the prostitute hadn't made it into the paper yet. It wouldn't hit the front page, anyway, he thought cynically.

Walking out to his vehicle in the early afternoon, he brooded. The attack had been aimed at him as well as Ms. Adams, albeit not as directly.

There were people who didn't like him, including

some in the police department. He was known for his unbending sense of right and wrong., which wasn't to say that he didn't understand why some cops ventured into the gray—he got as frustrated as anyone when he knew some piece of slime was walking because of a technicality, say, but vigilantism was as bad, in his opinion. He'd back an officer who'd momentarily lost his temper and said something impolitic, say, but had no patience when an act revealed arrogance or a bias.

In this case, if the original effort had actually resulted in a raid, it had been solely pointed at Alexa Adams. How serious the warning to him to butt out was…well, he'd find out.

This morning's newspaper article had made it clear that she wasn't backing down.

Getting into his police SUV, he couldn't help wondering when, not if, they'd go after her again, and whether she'd be seriously hurt or worse this time.

ALEXA'S PHONE VIBRATED, startling her. She was working at a secluded table in the branch library, one she was tempted to make a permanent claim on with a reserved sign. It was usually available anyway during hours when not many kids were around.

Although she'd hoped to hear from Diana Troxell, this caller was a fellow reporter at the *Tribune*. They had been consulting each other fairly often lately, since he worked the crime beat. Curious, she answered, keeping her voice low.

"Hey, there's a cop here looking for you," Greg Wells said. "Didn't know what to tell him."

She'd put in requests to interview half a dozen of the cops she was investigating, but they hadn't exactly yet leaped to volunteer for a chat, even with a union rep present. But to make their way into the *Tribune* building in search of her?

"Who is he?"

"Lieutenant Reinert." Gary's carefully neutral tone told her he knew very well who Reinert was.

Was this more of the nice guy who deeply regretted what had been done to her? Or had he been sent bearing a less friendly message? She gave a huff.

"I'm at the Madison branch library, working. If he wants to trek over, I should be here for another couple of hours."

After a murmur of voices, Gary said, "He says he's on his way unless he gets a callout."

Of course, her ability to concentrate was shot after that. She'd been reading everything she could uncover about a longtime scandal: the disappearance of drugs from the evidence locker at the county sheriff's office headquarters. Given that deputies had to check out any evidence borrowed—say, for court—and were theoretically on camera even when they wanted to look at a piece of evidence, the fact that someone had walked out unobserved with enough illegal drugs to sell for a nice side income should have triggered a bigger to-do than it so far had, in Alexa's opinion. To date, the sheriff and his spokespeople talked about inventory problems, how probably nothing had really disappeared.

Uh-huh. Alexa wondered what they'd say if, in a

spirit of civic high-mindedness, she offered to help with an inventory.

She managed to take a few notes, but wondering why Reinert wanted to talk to her again was a distraction. She'd have guessed that orders would have come down from on high for him *not* to talk to her.

Her view of the front blocked by tall shelving units packed with books, she didn't so much as hear a footstep before he appeared around one of those bookcases, expression quizzical.

"Hiding back here?" he asked.

And, blast it, his voice had enough texture to make goose bumps skitter down her spine.

He was dressed for the job in chinos, a dark green T-shirt and boots, the holstered handgun and badge at his waist making a real statement.

"That's the idea," she said, closing out her program before he could oh-so-casually circle the table to see what she was working on. "I concentrate best here. No interruptions."

His dark brows arched. "Is that a hint?"

"Oh." She was afraid her cheeks had flushed. "No, actually it wasn't."

"Good." He pulled out a chair and sat facing her, as relaxed as if he were lounging at his desk.

She decided to go for blunt. "What do you want?"

"Thought you'd like to be updated on my investigation."

"You'd really tell me if you find out which of your peers attacked me?"

Those dark eyebrows twitched.

Okay, she'd sounded as incredulous as she felt.

She went on. "Your chief and the city attorney haven't ordered a lockdown on communications yet?"

"Not to my knowledge," he said easily, his gaze never wavering from her face. "I think you're entitled."

She was, but hearing him say so blew her away. "So? What have you learned?"

His expression darkened. "Nothing. Nothing at all. We still can't find Jim Berkey, which makes me uneasy."

"You think…?"

"Probably he's just gone to ground. But, uh, he left an earlier tip that was aimed at you, too, although it took us a while to realize that."

"What?" Even having him share this much information stunned her. "Are you going to give me the details?"

"I can't. I shouldn't have said that much. I will say I was the one who shut down any consequences of the false tip."

What kind of consequences was he talking about? Had she been accused of a crime?

"Thus the message to you.".

"And the much stronger one to you."

"'Back off or else'?"

"Hard to read it any other way."

She could tell there was something he seemed reluctant to say, but she only nodded.

"Well, thank you for the report."

"Nice spread in the newspaper."

Alexa smiled. "Thank you. I was pleased with it."

That had to be amusement glinting in those gray eyes now. "Don't suppose you're backing off?"

Was that really what he wanted to know? Chilled, she said, "Not a chance."

Reinert nodded but didn't say anything for a minute. Something in the way he surveyed her felt personal—male-female—instead of having anything to do with the topic of conversation. Finally, confirming her suspicion, he said, "I'd suggest we go get a cup of coffee, but if I'm seen consorting with you, that might cause a problem."

"I'll bet it would," she agreed. Weirdly, she felt an unfamiliar buzz of excitement. He was unnervingly good-looking; how could she not admire his broad shoulders and long, muscular body? If his independence in coming to talk to her was honest, that attracted her, too. And she liked the hint of laughter she'd seen in his eyes and quirking one corner of his mouth.

"I'll let you get back to work." He pushed back the chair and rose to his feet. So big, she felt a momentary cramp of fear until she remembered the careful way he'd crouched in front of her in that alley to wrap her in his coat, shielding her from other eyes.

Expression troubled, he said, "As I said last time we talked, I encourage you to be cautious, Ms. Adams. Paranoia is an occupational hazard in my profession, but I don't think it's unreasonable to wonder if there'll be another salvo fired at you."

Her throat tightened. "Wouldn't that be taking a big chance, for whoever is behind this?"

"Yeah, they have to feel you snapping at their heels. They might be getting a little desperate if they know you're likely to come across something that will bring them down."

He took a business card out of a pocket and tossed it on top of her laptop, even though he'd already given her one as well as his phone number. "In case you tore the first one up," he said, his lips twitching. "Call me if anything makes you nervous." Then he nodded without waiting for her response and walked away, vanishing around the bookcase.

Alexa picked up the card and studied it. Would she dare call a cop to rescue her from another cop? She didn't know…but this time she'd go so far as to put him on speed dial.

MATTHEW LOOKED UP at the rap on his door. Vice detective Phil Banuelos stuck his head in without waiting for a response. "Got a minute?"

"If you have answers, I want to hear them."

It was Banuelos who should have thoroughly investigated Berkey's original tip. Obviously feeling defensive still, the first thing he said was, "You know that damn tip didn't come through me."

A patrol officer had passed on the message, unusual in that his few dealings with Jim Berkey, the CI, had been casual. Why would Berkey have chosen a cop he barely knew to pass on important information?

"You did vouch for the sleazeball," Matthew pointed out.

"The information he gives us is usually good." He hesitated. "Can I hear the call to the journalist again?"

Matthew pulled it up on his laptop and let it play, not liking the mumble or the street noise—traffic, voices that rose and fell, shouts—that made words indistinct.

The dark-haired detective leaned forward, absolutely intent. Then he slouched back in the chair. "Almost has to be him. That he's gone under now makes me nervous." He paused. "I wish I'd tried to reach him after the drug house tip."

Matthew gritted his teeth. Banuelos should have done a lot more than that, like some basic research or set up surveillance that would have immediately nipped the whole thing in the bud.

"Thing is, I'd been talking to him about this particular crowd. Pushing a little, you know. When I'm dogged enough, he comes through sometimes."

The hint of apology in the other detective's voice had Matthew rolling his shoulders to try to loosen the tension that would crawl up his neck and give him a headache if he let it. As ticked as he was at Banuelos, he knew how overworked he was.

"You didn't stop by for this," he said abruptly. "You have something else on your mind?"

"One of my detectives says he's been told that the drug gang was never in Wilden. He's trying to trace the original rumor on the street, but so far with no luck."

Yeah, there was a surprise.

Chapter Six

"The reaction was about what you'd expect," Diana told Alexa. Both had assumed they'd get some kind of response today from city and county entities. "Every single one of 'em is shocked by the suggestion that this 'incident'—that's the word of the day—is in any way their responsibility," the attorney continued. "Nobody in either department would consider *threatening* a journalist. That the thought even crossed your mind is absurd. Still, they deeply regretted that your assailants tried to convince you they were cops."

Alexa snorted. "As Detective Reinert put it, I'm obviously paranoid."

Still working from the library, Alexa had packed up her laptop and files and gone outside for this conversation. A few people had passed by since she'd settled on the handsome bench under a maple tree, but nobody was within earshot now.

"He's been in touch with you?" The attorney sounded horrified. "And he said something like that? I'm going to fry his ass—"

"No, no," Alexa hastened to say. "He did stop by

to talk this afternoon, supposedly to update me on his attempt to figure out how things went so wrong. Without being willing to give me details, he told me there'd been an earlier shot fired at me that he'd shut down. Thus the annoyed note aimed at him. I do think his real intent was to warn me to be cautious. That's when he said he's probably paranoid, but it's an occupational hazard. And maybe that's true, but he made it clear that he doesn't believe the company line you're describing, or that whoever is threatening me is finished."

There was a moment of silence. "It's…unusual he'd communicate with you the way he has."

"I think he may be sincere," Alexa heard herself say. And she was the original skeptic.

"Don't get too trusting," her lawyer warned.

"Me?"

Diana laughed then went on to tell her that she'd informed them she was preparing to file a lawsuit, and felt sure the details Alexa had described in her article would be persuasive to a jury.

"They tiptoed around a concession that a payout might be possible as long as they didn't have to admit to any culpability for your unpleasant experience. They just want this to go away, of course. That discussion might have gone further, say, to specific numbers, if I hadn't said that what you were asking for was open access to public records for the purpose of researching police officers suspected of conduct the public should know about."

She sounded exceptionally cheerful. "I said there's

no reason the staff should be so overwhelmed that it can take months to a year to supply information they are legally obligated to make public. That we suspect the recent rule change limiting requests is aimed at *you*, because they know they have an embarrassing number of officers in their departments who should never have been hired or who should have been fired for behavior on the job here in our own city."

Alexa laughed. "And?"

"They're outraged. Almost every police officer ends up being the subject of an occasional complaint from the public. There are people who dislike them, who don't understand how difficult the job they do is, who misunderstand what was happening in front of them although it's understandable that it appeared disturbing."

"Uh-huh."

"Don't worry. I won't let up. Your ears should be burning right now. I'll bet you're the subject of whole lot of conversations among the upper echelon in both police departments as well as the city and county. We'll see what they offer in response to my demands."

"Nothing we'll want to accept," Alexa said dryly.

"Not a chance. I'll keep you informed."

Alexa sat enjoying the sunlight for a few minutes. She had a bad tendency to hole up inside when she got obsessed with a particular investigation. She'd read about work/life balance, but didn't give it a thought most of the time. Maybe if she had a partner...

Yeah, her average was three or four dates before the guy realized that she was a modern-day, female

Don Quixote, so determined to tilt at windmills she wasn't about to let anything or anyone get in the way.

This wasn't the first time it had occurred to her that she might have a lot in common with cops in general, and especially detectives. They might get her, and her them.

Too bad she'd met so many who were supercharged and macho with a tendency to swagger. They came with their own problems, the kinds that led to substance abuse and or troubled relationships.

Wouldn't you know, a picture of Lieutenant Matthew Reinert appeared in her head, as it had too often this week. Looking too good to be believable.

She walked to her car, thinking about dinner. She hadn't defrosted anything this morning, but she could cook something simple like black bean quesadillas.

A couple of turns and she reached the main drag. Temptation momentarily called to her when she passed her favorite pizza restaurant, but she resolutely continued, braking when traffic slowed ahead of her.

A siren *whooped* right behind her, making her levitate. What the heck?

The marked city police car crowded her bumper, the rack of roof lights flashing.

Had she forgotten to signal or—

She heard Detective Reinert saying, *I don't think it's unreasonable to wonder if there'll be another salvo fired at you.* Was that what this was?

Alexa turned into the parking lot for an auto parts store and came to a stop. The police car rolled right up behind her.

Hands shaking, she shifted into Park and put on the emergency brake. For what seemed like forever, the officer behind the wheel just sat there. Trying to scare her?

No, probably looking her up for any priors, she reminded herself. Didn't squad cars have a computer now so he didn't have to call in for information?

In her side mirror, she saw that at last the officer was climbing out of his car. His hand rested on the butt of his gun as he walked forward. Wait—she should've gotten out her license and registration. She hastily took the folder from the glove compartment that held the registration.

A knock on her window made her jump.

Alexa rolled it down. "I don't understand why you stopped me, but—" She reached for her purse on the passenger seat.

His voice whipped out. "Hands on the steering wheel! Now! Do it!"

Completely rattled, she let the wallet drop back into the purse and started to comply. Before she could, the barrel of a gun was inches from her face.

"What are you *doing*?"

"Out of the car!" He wrenched open the door and grabbed her shoulder, which hurt on top of her recent injuries. Of course, her seat belt kept her in place. Next thing she knew, he was leaning over her, his breath bad, that gun pressed into her cheek. With the seat belt unfastened, he pulled her out of the car. She fell to her still-tender hands and knees on the gritty asphalt. People were staring, she knew that, but she didn't have room for humiliation right now, only now-too-familiar fear.

"I don't understand," she tried to say.

"On your feet!"

His hands were so rough as he wrenched her to her feet, she was going to have new bruises to go with the old. He planted her against her car, face pressing the back seat window.

"Hands against the car! Keep 'em there!"

Oh God. What was happening? Why?

He held a gun on her. She might have a print in her cheek from the barrel. If his finger tightened…

Was he one of the cops she was investigating? In this position, she couldn't possibly see his name.

"Why did you stop me?" she cried. "Why are you treating me like this?"

A handcuff snapped closed around her wrist and, before she knew it, he'd yanked both arms behind her and fully cuffed her.

Terrified and mad, she yelled, "You have no reason to arrest me! None!"

"I pulled you over because your brake light is out," the cop said. "When I looked you up, your vehicle is highlighted with a warning that you're armed and dangerous."

"I'm dangerous, all right," she managed to rasp through gritted teeth. "I know my rights."

"I'm doing my job," he growled.

"My name is Alexa Adams. Call Lieutenant Matthew Reinert." Were those tears burning hotly in her eyes? She surely did hope not. "He said he'd come if something like this happened again."

"How do you know Reinert?"

The ridge along the top of the window had to be etching a line in her face. "You heard about the woman who was stripped and left tied up in an alley Friday night? That was me."

Silence.

"Give me a minute."

Would he really call? Apparently so, because over the noise of passing traffic on the street, she thought she heard the scuff of his feet as he walked a short distance away. *Please don't let the lieutenant be too busy to answer his phone.* But she heard the murmur of one side of a conversation. Eyes closed, she tried to eavesdrop but couldn't distinguish any words.

A minute later, he returned and said, "I'm going to let you sit down on the back seat of your car. If you'll straighten up…"

She did. He opened the door.

"You won't take the cuffs off?"

"Not until the lieutenant says it's okay."

He maneuvered her so that she could sit sideways on the seat, her feet on the pavement. Her shoulders had already begun to ache. She stared at the officer, who'd backed up a couple of steps. So she couldn't tackle him with one lunge? This was the first time she'd really been able to see him.

He had to be early thirties. His head was shaved. He had a square face, a short, thick neck, and the shoulders of someone who spent a lot of time beefing up. There was nothing friendly or sympathetic in his eyes as he stared back at her.

The name pin on his pocket said…something Jackman. She thought. Not a name she'd come across before, although that didn't mean he didn't support his fellow officers who, say, felt justified in roughing up suspects. And, she'd surely be doing some research on him.

"You that reporter?" he said after a minute.

"Yes, I am."

"Why would you want to blacken the names of a lot of good men?" He sounded genuinely puzzled.

"Aren't there any good women in the police department?" she asked.

He obviously didn't get her point. Alexa let her head sag forward.

Please, Lieutenant, please don't be too far away. Please hurry.

MATTHEW DID A lot of swearing as he steered around stopped cars and hit his lights when he needed to cross an intersection. He was still grappling with the implications of that call. Ms. Adams's automobile license had been tagged to ensure the next cop who set eyes on it would pull her over, and not be polite after they did so.

How in *hell*—

Yeah, stupid question. Something told him getting an answer wouldn't be any easier than finding out how she'd been targeted for the raid that hadn't happened or the assault that had. But, man, whoever this was hadn't wasted any time. Maybe because they'd found out that she didn't want money in recompense for their mistake, she wanted access to any personnel records she asked to see.

That, of course, she was entitled to request and read. Hardly anybody who worked for the government—local or statewide—really grasped the concept of public records. Of what it meant to be an employee of the taxpayers.

He hit his siren again and maneuvered through a tangle of vehicles until he worked his way free enough to accelerate. The auto parts store was three blocks away. He covered the distance in a minute or less, turning in and pulling up right next to Alexa's car. The lights on the squad car still flashed, with the result that anyone in the parking lot or passing was sure to gape.

Matthew stopped abruptly enough that his SUV rocked. He hardly noticed as he leaped out and stalked around the front bumper of her vehicle until he saw Officer Jackman looking a little uneasy as he guarded the open door of her car.

Her head came up. The dark hair she usually wore in a smooth knot at her nape had come undone. He'd seen the turmoil in her eyes before. Relief might be mixed with the anger and fear this time. He'd like to think so.

"You cuffed her?" he said incredulously.

"It said 'armed and dangerous,'" Jackman mumbled.

Matthew let loose with an expletive and bent over

Alexa. "Damn, I'm sorry. Here, let me—" He used his key to free one of her wrists, then the other when it fell to her side.

"You came." This expression was almost naked. She hadn't believed him when he'd said he would.

"I keep promises," he said tersely. "I didn't expect to have to this soon."

"Me, neither." She actually tried to smile, although it was so shaky he couldn't be positive what she'd intended.

He crouched inside the V of the door to be at her level. "Did he hurt you? Do anything I need to know about?"

Her gaze flickered past him to Jackman then back to his face. "I...think I'll have bruises, but only because he yanked me out of the car, and I fell to my hands and knees." She held out her hands, skinned and with some grit clinging. "And..." This time she bit her lip. "He pulled his gun on me. Put it right in my face." Deep breath. "But I guess he had reason to think I was a threat."

He mumbled a word under his breath he hoped she didn't make out. "Where were you going?"

"Home." She made a sound.

Damn, he hoped she was safe there, at least. "Can you drive?"

She obviously gave his question some thought, finally nodding. "It's not that far."

"I'll follow you."

"I warn you, I'm calling my attorney."

Matthew met her eyes straight-on. "You should."

Her head bobbed. "Can I go now?"

"Give me just a minute, okay?"

He rose and walked around behind her car. After a moment, he gestured the other cop over. Jackman joined him in studying the brake light, which wasn't just "out." It had been smashed.

"Looks like someone used a boot," Jackman said uneasily. "Or a rock."

"This wasn't chance. She was set up," Matthew said grimly. "Again."

Jackman cleared his throat. "Yeah, it, uh, kind of looks like it."

Matthew took out his phone and snapped several photos of the damage; a couple that included her license plate. Then, shaking his head, he returned to Alexa, holding out a hand. She gaped at it for a minute as if not understanding why it was hovering there in front of her. Then, tentatively, she laid her hand in his and he tugged her to her feet, being careful not to put any stress on her shoulders or hurt her sore palm.

"Thank you," she mumbled.

He closed the back door of her car and opened the driver's door. Yeah, her keys were still in the ignition, her purse on the seat. A piece of paper had fallen to the floorboard. He picked it up to see that it was the registration for the car. He laid it beside her purse and backed away, letting her get in before closing the door. No question she already knew this wasn't an honest mistake, but he'd wait until they reached her house before he showed her the smashed light.

She put on her seat belt and started the car, but when

he turned away to have more words with Jackman, Alexa just sat there. Collecting herself, he guessed.

As he walked to his vehicle, she finally started forward, aiming for an exit from the parking lot. Within minutes, he'd snugged up right behind her on the four-lane road. He always stayed aware when he was driving—and most of the rest of the time, too, but now his gaze flicked nonstop: rearview mirror, in front of him, one side-view mirror then the other. Businesses fronting the road, every other damn car on it. He felt like he did before closing in for an arrest with the expectation that things would go south. Tense, trying to figure out what might go wrong, seeing things that weren't there.

Only this time, the adrenaline didn't translate into excitement. Dread might be a better word.

As he'd expected, whoever had masterminded the campaign to scare off Ms. Adams wasn't done. As ugly and humiliating as the original assault had been, this had had the potential to be as dangerous. Jumpy enough to pull his gun, Jackson had been a hair from actually pulling the trigger. If Alexa had taken something from her purse that he'd even momentarily thought might be a weapon—say, her phone—he could have tightened his finger. Fired.

Killed her.

Somebody had a real hate on, and this episode made it a certainty that he was a cop. Matthew wished he were making any progress whatsoever in figuring out who that faceless piece of garbage was.

He was going down, but Matthew had to keep

Alexa alive and unscathed until that happened. Something told him she wouldn't be willing to take a nice long vacation, or back off on her investigations for now.

No, once the fear receded, she'd be madder than ever. He'd feel the same—but he was more afraid for her than he'd have been for himself.

Chapter Seven

Alexa sat on a stool at her breakfast bar, fingers knotted together as she listened for the occasional sound as a cop did a walk-through of her house. A cop who *seemed* sincere, but…how was she to know?

Would her executive editor agree to run an article insisting that she was just one reporter, that if she was deterred or killed, ten others would take her place, swarming the two law enforcement agencies? Would whoever felt threatened by her believe that if he read it?

And…was it even true? Sure, she had the full support of her editors, but this was her crusade. Her idea to write a series of articles on problem officers and the consequences of letting them stay on the job. If the public couldn't trust the men in uniform, they needed to know that.

A door down the hall opened then a moment later softly closed. Closet doors slid on their tracks in what had to be her bedroom. She hadn't left anything out in her home office that she shouldn't, had she?

Damn. Why was she just sitting there? She should have already called her attorney.

When Matthew walked quietly back into the kitchen a minute later, Alexa was explaining the latest to Diana, who was furious.

"I can clear my schedule at nine tomorrow if that isn't too early for you. We need to strategize again. There's no way they can deny this traffic stop happened, is there?"

"No." Alexa discovered she had a lump in her throat. "At least…"

Matthew had his phone in his hands, and hers pinged.

"I sent you a few photos," he said.

"Just a minute," she said to Diana, and went to texts to see the pictures he'd forwarded. A couple of close-ups of her broken taillight, but also a photo that showed the squad car behind her, rack of lights still flashing, and Officer Jackman hovering near her bumper. Not really recognizable unless the photo was enlarged, and then she felt sure he would be.

"Thank you," she murmured, and explained to the attorney that she had pictures.

Once she set her phone down, she looked at Matthew, who was leaning against the kitchen counter, seemingly relaxed and even feeling at home. Of course, he had a holstered gun and badge on his belt, which made her wonder how fast he could move from that casual pose if he felt the need.

"Why are you helping?" she asked bluntly. "Can't you get in trouble for aiding and abetting the enemy?"

His eyes rose. "You're not the enemy. You aren't attacking law enforcement officers. If I understand right, your goal is to root out the ones who shouldn't be wearing a badge. Sometimes there's a fine line between an action that a civilian would jump on and the way a particular situation should ideally have been handled. We make mistakes, but that's not what we're talking about. If it was, I'd support my peers. The ones who enjoy beating up suspects, or blackmail women into servicing them sexually or violate the rules to punish an ex-wife's new boyfriend..." He shook his head. "When they're caught, they should be fired and, when appropriate, arrested. No hesitation. The complaints shouldn't disappear into the files, and we sure as hell shouldn't hire officers with serious complaints on their records from other departments. If you can persuade the public to press for change, I'm all for it."

She tipped her head and studied him. Heaven help her, she *liked* the deepened lines in his face that made him look like he shouldered a great deal in life. She would never have imagined being attracted to a cop, not given their usual image, but if this one was really being honest, that meant he cared. Physically... tall, rangy, with a strong-boned face and penetrating gray eyes, he pushed her buttons.

And he'd come racing, siren blaring and lights flashing, when she'd needed him.

"I should have thought to take these pictures." She nodded at her phone. "I let myself get rattled."

"Most people get a little shaken up when they've had to look down the barrel of a gun." He wasn't amused; his tone was grim. "Plenty of cops carry

Glocks that don't have a safety. The triggers are… sensitive. I don't think you're the only one who's rattled, by the way.

"Jackman is a good cop, as far as I know, and you can be damn sure he's seeing nightmare scenarios flashing before his eyes now. He was set up, in a different way than you were, and realizing how easily it happened—and could happen again—has to shake his confidence. That could make him hesitate when he shouldn't, but it'll also make him think twice when that's smart to do."

"I should hope so!" Alexa hesitated. "Do you, um, have time for a cup of coffee?"

"Tell you the truth, I'm getting hungry." He eyed her with what she thought might be wariness. "What I should do is wish you a good evening and leave."

Her heartbeat picked up speed.

"But I'm wondering whether you might like to go out together and get some dinner."

Just ask, she told herself. "Are you thinking we can keep talking about who might be behind these attacks on me and what we can do to flush him out? Or—"

He smiled, a little ruefully. "Or. Definitely or…"

SHE'D BEEN THE one to call in an order for a pizza and salads so they didn't have to go out. Matthew didn't comment, but Alexa figured he'd be relieved. Associating with a cop wouldn't make her automatically suspect among her peers, but a cop dating a journalist who was investigating his department? Really, she didn't understand why he wasn't politic enough to be avoiding her like the plague.

Except, she could guess. If she asked, he'd be arrogant enough to say that he didn't give a damn if he got called in by his chief for a butt-chewing. Well, he might be able to shrug that off, but she hated the idea of him getting fired. She'd be left hanging out there with no backup.

And, yes, being trusting enough to think of him that way came as a surprise to her, but how could she not?

He'd darned well better not have any vision of ending the evening in her bed, though. Her trust didn't stretch that far.

As it was, she was torn between wishing she'd just said no about dinner and being glad to have company. If they were really going to talk, at least this was better. No background music, he wouldn't have to stay hyperaware of his surroundings the way she'd heard cops tended to be. Nobody could eavesdrop, either. Still…part of her edginess had to do with the possibility he might kiss her goodnight. Or try, anyway. He'd expressed his interest bluntly.

They made stiff conversation until the doorbell rang. He insisted on answering the door, in case of an unpleasant surprise, and on signing the credit slip. Alexa didn't love his insistence on paying for the dinner, but all he did was raise his eyebrows and say, "Call me old-fashioned. I did the asking, I foot the bill."

By the time he returned to the kitchen with the

pizza and a bag presumably holding their salads, she'd already gotten out plates and napkins and poured herself some water.

"Would you like a beer?"

"Sure, but…what about you?" he asked.

She wrinkled her nose. "I don't like beer. Lucky for you, some friends left a couple in my fridge."

"Ah. Wine?"

"To tell you the truth, I'm not much of a drinker. I had a stepfather who was a raging alcoholic. It kind of left me with some scars, if you know what I mean."

"Yeah. I know."

His terse response ramped up her curiosity about him. Since she'd met one part of his family… "So, your brother—Nate, right?—is here in town. Does that mean your family is, too?"

"No. My parents split up a few years ago and Nate came to live with me. He graduated from high school here and is just finishing his AA degree at the community college."

"He didn't stay home until he finished high school?" None of her business, but the question just popped out.

"Home? Where was that? Anyway, it seemed as if Mom and Dad pretty much ditched Nate—" He grimaced.

"It must be almost as weird having your parents split up when you're an adult as when you're still home and in the middle of it."

Matthew seemed to be really good at suppressing

what she thought of as physical tells, but the way he rolled his shoulders gave away some discomfiture.

"In general, it's not as traumatic, I imagine," he said after a minute. "But my parents turned into strangers. I kept thinking, Wait! But no, Mom really said that, and yeah, he'd been screwing—" He stopped abruptly.

It was obvious he hadn't meant to say that much. Alexa lowered her guard enough to reach across the table and touch the back of his hand lightly. "You don't have to tell me about it."

His gaze dropped to her hand. "It's okay. That was only part of it. The worst was that neither of them saw what they were doing to Nate. They became unbelievably self-centered. I'm left wondering whether I was deceiving myself all those years. Did they really change that drastically, or did I just imagine my family was solid?"

"If you'd been younger, too—"

His expression closed. "I was glad I had the resources to take Nate in."

Wow. This felt unnervingly like a real date; one that had moved on with pedal-to-the-floor speed, too. Forget what movies or hobbies they liked—they'd gone right for the gut. Alexa couldn't seem to pull herself back, though.

Heck, she'd always been nosy. Why else become an investigative journalist? Supposedly, curiosity killed the cat, but she hadn't died yet.

Although, this past week, she'd come perilously

close—*twice*—and that had to be because of her nosiness.

This was innocuous, though. "Nate still lives with you?" she asked.

Matthew laughed. "No, he has an apartment with some friends. He's already been accepted to Washington State University and is thinking of going into chemical engineering."

"Not criminology?"

"When I suggested it, he laughed at me."

"Doesn't want to walk in his big brother's footsteps, huh?"

He sobered. "The honor, justice and public service police are supposed to embody hasn't been on the best display lately."

Perturbed, she said, "You don't take pride in what you do?"

Matthew released a long breath. "I do, but I'm finding myself looking around real uneasily of late."

It felt weird to be talking like this. Actually, it felt strange having Matthew—forget distancing him by calling him "lieutenant"—here in her house, sitting at her table in the small nook off the kitchen. He filled more space than should be possible, probably through sheer force of personality.

Although she couldn't discount the breadth of his shoulders, or his muscles, either.

Her cheeks felt warm. Hoping he hadn't noticed, she said, "You seem like a confident guy."

He set a half-eaten piece of pizza onto his plate. "I

am. Not being able to get answers about who is targeting you isn't bolstering my confidence, though."

Wiping her fingers on a napkin, she nodded. The things he'd said earlier, about how problem police officers should be handled, fit with this man's character, as she was beginning to see it. His expectations for himself would be high, and she bet he tried to hold the people around him to standards just as high. Was frustration the real reason he was sitting here, close enough that his knees were bumping hers? Not attraction. But his needing to earn her…what? Faith that he could keep her safe? Or did he want to hear her say, *None of this was your fault. Go in peace.*

Maybe.

He shook his head slightly, as if shaking off a disturbing subject.

"What about you? Are you a local?"

"Not even close. Can't you hear the accent?"

Wheels visibly turned. "Boston?"

"Close enough. I came out to the west coast for school. Speaking of confidence, I was filled with it until I had that degree in journalism and started looking for a job. In one way, I knew that newspapers were biting the dust right and left, but, naturally, some executive editor would recognize brilliance when he saw it and snap me up." Alexa made a face at her naïveté. Honestly, she couldn't have picked a worse time to launch her career.

Well, except for every one of the intervening years, when more and more newspapers went under.

"I didn't want some online gig, and television news

wasn't for me. I was incredibly lucky to be taken on here by the *Tribune*. Even luckier to have an editorial staff that eventually saw enough promise in me to turn me loose to pursue in-depth investigations. This kind of stuff can be expensive, in terms of the time it takes to produce results and—" she grinned "—the risk of lawsuits."

Matthew laughed. "Yet here you are, threatening to file your own lawsuits."

"Sometimes, it's the only way to get results."

"Can't argue."

They ate for a minute without either saying anything. She kept wondering about him.

"You must have worked construction at some point," she remarked.

"Nope. Don't I wish." He smiled at her expression. "I bought a house a couple of years ago. Built in 1910. Big-time fixer upper. I thought it might be fun."

Her turn to laugh. "I've had friends who bought old houses that had, in theory, already been renovated. They say there's still one headache after another."

"I can only hope to get to that stage. Right now, it's more like backaches, bruises, a broken collarbone when a wall collapsed on me, and constant bewilderment. Before I start any project, I have to teach myself how to do it first."

Alexa enjoyed the humor in his voice and on his face. Not everybody could laugh at themselves. "I take it you've replaced some doors."

"No, no, no. I took the doors down, stripped them,

repainted or refinished them, replaced hardware and rehung them. Doors, I have down pat. I'm feeling good about plumbing. Spackling, I'm a champ." He shook his head. "The only thing I've hired out is replacing the wiring. Electricity scares me."

She nodded. "For good reason. I've written about some house fires. Remember the one where the baby was killed?"

"Yeah. I know the mother. She works in the DA's office. She and her husband haven't tried for another child. It's been—what?—three years."

"Something like that." She frowned. "I'm surprised I haven't run into you before."

"We might have been in the same courtroom or someplace like that before. I've read your stuff, and you're now famous in the police department."

"Don't you mean infamous?"

He laughed again, his eyes glinting. "I was being polite."

"It's a little late for that."

Every trace of humor left his face. After a moment, he asked, "Am I tarred with the same brush? Are you trying to tell me this isn't happening?" His gesture encompassed the two of them.

MATTHEW WAS STILL brooding about her answer Wednesday while he pretended to be absorbed in the test results that would determine promotions within the department. His division was below strength, so he should be jumping on this. Instead, he kept seeing that moment yesterday evening.

Alexa had stared at him for longer than he'd liked, then taken a deep breath and said with what felt like painful honesty, "I don't know. I'm…a little off cops right now. And…not very good at trust at the best of times."

Which this wasn't. He got that. Now, he regretted having laid his feelings on the table. He felt sure the undercurrent of sexual attraction had been going both ways, that her interest in his family and background had been a good sign. The sense of intimacy had taken him by surprise, but some instinct had pushed him to open up to her more than he usually would on a first date. Not "some instinct." He'd seen her at some seriously low moments. The only hope of achieving any balance had been in baring his vulnerable underside.

A rap on his door yanked him back to the present. "Come in."

Art Dwyer walked in. "Got a few minutes?"

"Of course I do." He waved at the chairs on the other side of his desk.

Art took a seat. "Did you hear about that stop Ward and O'Brien made last week? They claimed to think the guy was going for a gun?"

Damn, this wasn't about Berkey. Since Dwyer was working a dozen active cases, that wasn't a surprise.

"I heard. I can't say I know either of them, except—" He looked at the list of names and test scores displayed on his monitor. "Jim Ward?"

"Yeah."

"He took the exam for a promotion."

Dwyer grimaced.

"Don't worry. He scored near the bottom of this bunch."

"Good, because I have a lot of concerns about him. Yesterday, I surprised him and a couple of his friends when I came out a door right by their huddle in the hall. They were smirking and laughing about roughing up a guy they'd hoped was an illegal."

Matthew shook his head, not in disbelief but in disgust. He'd already heard at least some of the follow-up. "The witnesses with their cell phones tripped them up."

"And the fact that their victim was a US citizen born in this country."

Matthew grunted. "How is he? Do you know?"

"Released from the hospital. They kept him overnight because of the concussion. He has multiple broken ribs, broken cheekbone, forearm—from the clip I saw, he was trying to protect his face—and his nose is a mess."

Matthew swore pungently. "Tell me Ward and O'Brien are on suspension." That, he hadn't heard.

"Initially, no. Once the *Tribune* and our local TV news channels got some of the cell phone footage and raised a stink, the two were pulled off the street while an investigation is conducted."

"But from what you overheard, they still don't think there'll be any consequences."

"Can you blame them?" Dwyer ran a hand over the thinning hair on top of his head. "King County fired O'Brien four years ago for a seemingly unprovoked assault on a homeless man. The complaints since we snapped him up are legion. Ward less so, but he was on a prostitute sting—"

Matthew's phone rang. He'd have let the caller go if it had been almost anyone else. "It's Carrera," he told Art. "Detective in the sheriff's department. Do you know him? He heard about our interest in Berkey and thought he had a lead." The only hint of a lead so far.

Art stretched out his legs and waited, head cocked in interest.

Matthew answered his phone. "News?"

"One of our informants says he knows where Berkey is right now. The house is outside the city limits. You free to join me?"

Matthew opened his mouth to give eager agreement, but had to close it. He was supposed to accompany one of his rookie detectives to interview several persons of interest in a murder. Teaching, overseeing, had become increasingly big parts of his job with each promotion.

Yeah, but this was that SOB Berkey. And Art had worked harder than Matthew had to get his hands on the tipster. He deserved in on this.

"Hold on a sec," Matthew said into the phone, then explained quickly to Art.

"Hell, yes, I want to be there!" Matthew's friend and fellow detective jumped to his feet as Matthew told Carrera he was sending Dwyer instead. Art took Matthew's phone long enough for the two men to arrange where to meet up.

Returning the phone, Art said, "I need to run. Lay-ing our hands on Berkey has to be a priority right now. The rest of what I stopped by to say can wait. It's the prostitute angle—" He shook his head. "I'll let you know what we find."

Left alone again, Matthew sank reluctantly back into his desk chair and did battle with the desire to run after his fellow detective and say, *Forget about it. I'm on this.*

If there was anyone in the department he trusted, bone deep, it was Art Dwyer.

And what had he meant by "the prostitute angle"? Murders, yes, but "angle"?

Chapter Eight

Alexa had spent her day so far diving eagerly into the spate of records and—yes!—even some body camera footage that both the city and county had released in a not-so surprising burst of compliance. It had taken her a couple of hours to realize that she'd been given the least damaging material she'd requested. Yeah, she didn't like some of the conduct she was seeing, but most of it wouldn't make it into her article. Or series. She didn't yet know which.

Matthew hadn't had to tell her that cops were human; they panicked and made a bad decision, or suddenly cracked when someone pushed the right button, and kept pushing. That was to be expected. Handled in-house, preferably resulting in more training or counseling. A suspension at worst.

She watched again as a woman rose on tiptoe so she could get into a cop's face to scream at him in a voice that made Alexa think of fingernails on a good, old-fashioned blackboard. He stayed patient, giving the admittedly vague answer that was also the only one he could offer, six or seven times before his impassive face gave way to anger and he said some re-grettable things.

No, he shouldn't have. But what he'd done wasn't close to the ugly behavior that Alexa was digging deep to find.

Sighing, she moved to the next file then decided to pour herself a cup of coffee first.

Her phone rang while she was in the kitchen, so she had to backtrack. Matthew Reinert was calling, she saw. With mixed feelings, she answered. "Hey. Did you learn something?"

There was a pause. "About who set you up? No, although it looks like we may put our hands on Jim Berkey. I'm tied up and couldn't go, but I sent Detective Dwyer. I have faith in him. Right now, I'm just waiting."

"This Berkey might not be willing to talk." The side of right and order was unlikely to be nearly as frightening as her two assailants. Alexa could speak to that.

"We'll see." He paused. "I have someone digging into the origin of the 'armed and dangerous' designation on your car, too, but she's not getting anywhere, either. At the moment, I'm just…checking in. Making sure you're okay," he said in the voice that might as well have been a touch.

Thank goodness, he wasn't there to *see* her bare toes curl. "I'm working from home today. I've got to tell you, I'm tempted to rent a car for a while, so I'm not such an obvious target."

"That's actually not a bad idea."

"You're serious?" she said incredulously.

"Given that traffic stop? Damn straight I am." He sounded affronted. "That's assuming, of course, that nobody is actually keeping an eye on your house."

Because if someone was, driving a different car would do her no good. That's what he was saying.

"Surely nobody in Dispatch would buy another sudden tip saying I'm armed and dangerous."

"Probably not, but word doesn't always get to everyone it should."

"Did I mention that print journalists don't make big salaries?"

He laughed. "Have I mentioned that cops don't, either?"

"My point," she said with dignity, "is that renting a car for what might turn out to be weeks isn't in my budget. I'd rather spend that money on a midwinter vacation. Sunshine, turquoise waters, golden sand beach…"

"Which you can't enjoy if you're dead," he said bluntly.

"Was this call meant to cheer me up?"

"I did mean to be supportive," he admitted. "Mostly… I wanted to hear your voice."

She went very still. That wasn't the cop speaking. It was the man. He sounded as if he was on edge, maybe because he really believed Berkey would give them some answers. He had to know that she wouldn't be able to consider having any kind of relationship with him—and he'd been up-front about having that in mind—as long as a good part of his department was made up of her antagonists.

Or…he was facing some kind of danger? But how likely was that? From what she could gather, the average detective spent as much time as she did on the phone and computer rather than pull out his or her gun and chase down suspects. Matthew had administrative responsibilities besides.

Maybe not being able to go after Berkey himself was rubbing him the wrong way.

Still… "You're being careful, too, aren't you?" she said as an alternative to all the other things that had crossed her mind. "I'm not the only person those guys are mad at."

"I'm looking at that as a positive. I might never have met you if not for the note left with you."

Did she hear a smile? Her heart threw in an extra uncomfortable beat.

Given all her doubts, she sidestepped the implication. "Will you let me know what you find out?"

"I will. But you keep being careful, Alexa." And then he was gone.

SEEING THE NAME on the screen, Matthew snatched up his phone and pushed back from the desk. "Carrera?"

"It's Art!" The unfailingly even-tempered detective sounded distraught. "He was shot. He…doesn't look good."

"*What?*"

"He went to the back door, I knocked on the front. Heard firing out back, ran around. Art was down. It was a headshot, Reinert. He's alive, but— Just a minute." Carrera talked to someone else then came back. "We think the shooter was in the alley, close enough to use a handgun. An ambulance is on the way. Do you have his wife's number?"

"Yes. I'll call her. Art isn't conscious?" He knew better, but had to ask.

"No." Carrera's swallow was audible. "I hope that siren is the ambulance. Listen, I gotta go. More units have responded. Shooter is probably long gone, but—"

"Berkey?"

"House appears to be vacant. This was a setup."

"Another setup," Matthew said grimly.

"Yeah." Carrera ended the call.

Feeling sick, Matthew scrolled to Art's home number and hit Call.

Michelle answered on the second ring. Matthew knew she always kept her phone close. Maybe she'd spent twenty years expecting this call.

"Matthew?"

"Art's been shot. He's on his way to the hospital."

"He's alive?" Her voice shook.

"I wasn't with him. I'm told he was shot in the head and is unconscious."

"Oh God." She was quiet for a bare instant then exclaimed, "I have to go. I have to be there!"

"I'm on my way, too—" But he realized he was talking to dead air.

He beat her to the hospital, for what good that did. The ambulance had arrived just ahead of him. Nobody with any real information had time to talk to him. Five minutes later, Michelle ran in, gaze frantically searching until it locked on him.

He gripped her arms when she reached him. "I don't know any more yet. They're too busy working on him to come out and talk."

She whimpered and he wrapped his arms around her. About Art's age, she'd fed Matthew a few hundred meals, even plied a paintbrush a few times at his house, and they'd become good friends. He wasn't surprised when she didn't let herself lean on him for long, though.

"I should call Steph. She'd want to be here."

Their fifteen-year-old daughter.

"Why don't we wait?" he suggested gently. "Until we get some word?"

If Art was dead—Matthew didn't even want to think about it. Art's family would be devastated. It would take time for his boy to get home from college. Stephanie wasn't at a good age to handle this kind of devastation. Finances— No, he had to believe Art would have made sure they were okay.

As if that worry was at the top of anybody's mind.

He walked her up to the counter, where she gave the receptionist info including health insurance number, allergies, et cetera. Then all they could do was wait.

After what felt like an eternity, Carrera called.

Glancing at Michelle, who was staring straight ahead and probably seeing nothing, Matthew walked away before answering.

Voice flat, Carrera said, "We didn't find anything.

An old man at the corner heard a car start close by not long after the gunshot, but he's slow on his feet and by the time he got to the window, the car was gone. Assuming he'd have been able to see it from his front window anyway."

"The house?"

"No indication anyone has been living there, or even just squatting. Neighbors say it's been empty for a while. They know the landlord and think he's short of cash. Can't afford to fix the house up, no one will rent it in such lousy condition."

Matthew didn't care about the house, but the questions had had to be asked. You never knew what passing tidbit would provide the all-important lead.

"I don't know if it's occurred to you yet," the other detective said, "but I can't help wondering if *you* weren't supposed to be the victim. Everyone in both our departments knows who's the driving force behind the investigation into what happened with the reporter woman, and that you're determined to get your hands on Berkey. They'd have had good reason to think you'd walk right into their ambush."

The thought had crossed Matthew's mind, but he found himself shaking his head. "They also have to know that I spend most of my time behind the desk these days, that delegating is my job."

"Everyone is saying you've been taking this stuff personally."

Oh good. Nice to know he was the subject of intense gossip—and that he'd been transparent despite his usual impassive demeanor.

"I have taken offense, you're right about that," he admitted. "But anyone watching for me couldn't have mistaken Art for me. If they were after me, why shoot him?"

Noticeably dropping his voice, Carrera said, "If the shooter was a cop? Sure. Everyone knows Dwyer. *And* what good friends you are. This could have been another message for you."

That note flashed before Matthew's inner eye, chilling him. *Lieutenant Reinert, you should have been smart and stayed out of it.*

He'd ignored instructions. In doing so, had he killed his best friend?

Or had Art been the real target because *he* was the one heading the hunt for Jim Berkey? Something else every cop within the city and county would know.

After ending the call, he walked back to Michelle, who was watching him. As he dropped into the seat beside her, she asked, "How did this happen?"

She was a cop's wife, and he wasn't going to lie to her.

She looked almost numb as he told her as much as he felt he could.

"Mrs. Art Dwyer…?" a voice called.

"Heard someone talking at the courthouse," Diana Troxell said. "I'm still there, in the ladies' room right now."

It hadn't surprised Alexa to hear from Diana; they had been talking regularly. This was different, though. Something about the hushed voice told her that whatever the attorney had overheard, Alexa wouldn't like it.

Clutching her cell phone, she asked, "What did you hear?"

"A cop's been shot. It doesn't sound good."

Alexa felt as if she'd just stepped off the edge of a cliff. She'd start falling any second. "Wilden PD?"

"Yes, but when I tried to find out who, nobody would say." There was a murmur of voices in the background. Presumably, Diana was no longer alone in the restroom. "I've got to go," she said hurriedly. "I'll let you know if I hear more, and if it has anything to do with you."

All Alexa could think was, What if Matthew was dead?

No, that was surely unlikely. But there'd been that unsettling *something* in his voice when he'd called. The death of a detective working under him would impact him, which meant it mattered to Alexa. Realizing how true that was came as a shock. Her feelings for him should be a lot more mixed than they were.

I could fall in love with him, she thought, looking down at the cell phone she still held.

Oh, dear God, what if he'd been killed? Nobody would tell *her*, even if he had been shot pursuing a lead that had to do with the attacks on her. She could track down his brother, but the obvious step was just to call Matthew. Since she'd entered his number in her phone, she didn't even have to hunt for it.

If he didn't answer… Well, there were lots of reasons he might not, especially in the aftermath of such a disaster. She couldn't assume anything. But she knew she wouldn't be able to concentrate on anything else until he called back.

Which he'd do. Of course he would.

ONCE ART HAD been moved to ICU, first his wife then Matthew had been allowed in to see him.

Standing beside the bed, Matthew swore under his breath as he gazed down at the stocky man who looked dead except for the fact that his chest rose and fell with each breath. He was breathing on his own; that was good news, the doctor had said. His head was heavily bandaged. Matthew had asked where the bullet struck and noted that it had been low enough, it might have been aimed at his neck. A few inches lower, that bullet would have torn through Art's neck and throat, probably opening the carotid artery.

Just as it had Tansy Gould's.

Coincidence? Or not? Good shot? Or a miss? Matthew asked himself. The shooter would have assumed Art was wearing a vest.

As it was, the bullet had ricocheted off Art's head, but had shattered his skull where it struck. He was officially in a coma; they'd drained fluid from his brain and were monitoring him closely.

"At this point," the doctor had said, after clearing his throat, "we can't tell you what to expect. He could open his eyes a few hours from now, or remain in a coma for an unknown length of time."

He didn't say, *Or slip away*, but Michelle and Matthew both heard the unspoken words.

Michelle would be allowed to sit with her husband for intervals. She made the decision to update her daughter with calls but not let her see her father like this.

Looking shell-shocked, Michelle called the mother of a friend of Stephanie's, who would pick her up at school, and then phoned their son, Brian, at the University of Washington.

She'd intended to tell him to stay at school until they knew more, but Brian wouldn't have it. Matthew was to pick him up at the airport. He was glad; Michelle was forgetting that *she'd* need support, too.

He couldn't kid himself. A fellow cop had shot Art. Had to be. This felt like a nightmare, so many things going wrong in his department. He'd trusted most of the men and women with whom he served. That trust was quaking under his feet now, and he had to wonder whether the chief would have his back. He, his minions, and the city officials all seemed to want to sweep anything troublesome under the rug. What happened when he let them all know, from Internal Affairs to the police chief himself, that he felt certain someone wearing a badge had fired that bullet? Had set a trap and laid in patient wait to kill a long-serving member of the department—a good, kind, smart man?

Matthew had a feeling he was going to become a thorn digging into their bare flesh. He'd already resolved to uncover the truth of the lowlife dogging Alexa. He wouldn't relent in his pursuit of the piece of scum who'd shot Art, no matter who it turned out to be. If he was ordered to defend the department's reputation above all, his superiors were about to receive a shock.

And he was for damn sure going to give Art's wife both truth and justice, however cold the comfort that either offered.

A COUPLE OF hours later, Matthew sat at his desk, the door to his office closed. He felt paralyzed. Brian had let him know he wouldn't be able to fly in until morning and said he'd get an Uber to the hospital, which let Matthew concentrate on an investigation that had no obvious strings to pull.

They had no witness, no shell left at the scene. Fingerprints taken from the front and back doors of the house led nowhere. Why would the shooter have approached the house? He hadn't needed to.

Matthew called to check in with Michelle again. No change.

His job was to take a look at everything Art had been working on, not make assumptions despite the Berkey connection. Jim Berkey's name had been thrown around a lot lately. Someone who wanted Art dead for an unrelated reason might have heard the name, used it as a lure.

That meant, gut feeling aside, he couldn't rule out the possibility the shooter *wasn't* a cop.

So. Proceed on the assumption that Art had been targeted because of something he knew or suspected. Start by examining all his recent investigations, which Matthew would have to take over or reassign anyway. Temporarily, he wanted to believe, but he had no choice.

The last conversation they'd had right here in this office nibbled at Matthew. If only they hadn't been interrupted. Art had seemed worried. What was it he'd started to say?

They'd been talking about the traffic stop Ward and O'Brien had made, Matthew remembered, and the conversation Art had overheard. Those two officers were in serious trouble now, which they must know even if they'd been smirking for their buddies. What if one of them had said something that would increase their legal peril, and knew Art had overheard it?

Matthew shook his head. The traffic stop was already being scrutinized, body camera and cell phone footage available. Would anything said carelessly really make matters worse?

No, Art had been working his way up to a point. He'd said something about how Ward had been in on a prostitute sting—but Art hadn't had a chance to tell Matthew what had happened.

Matthew's jaw tightened. Dirty cops and prostitutes. That was the connection. And it so happened Art had been primary on the series of murders of local prostitutes—and his recent focus had been the latest murder: Tansy Elizabeth Gould's. What had he learned?

Suddenly energized, Matthew had just pushed back from his desk when his cell phone rang. Alexa.

He answered. "Hey."

"You're all right."

"You heard about the shooting," he said slowly.

"Only that…that a police officer was injured or killed. Diana—my attorney—heard talk at the courthouse."

He paused. "She heard right. I'm…dealing with the fallout," he said. "And trying to figure out what the hell happened."

"Was it…a patrol officer? Or someone you work closely with?"

He pinched the bridge of his nose. "He's a good friend. A detective, too, so we worked—work—together daily. He's in a coma. Right now, we just don't know…" His throat closed.

Damn. Surely, he'd piqued the journalist's interest.

But all she said was a soft, "I'm sorry."

"Thanks. I can't give you his name until the department is ready to release it."

"I wasn't trying to butter you up. I'm not on the crime beat."

"I know you're not." He hesitated. "Can I stop by this evening?"

She was quiet. "I was afraid it was you."

He waited.

"Yes. Yes, of course. If you want, I can make dinner."

"I'd like that," he said simply.

Chapter Nine

Knowing he'd see her this evening centered him in some way, helped him face his task of going through Art's desk, computer, phone—if he could figure out the password—and probably even his car.

Matthew was immediately reminded about Art's habit of scribbling notes to himself on random pieces of paper and scattering them behind him like confetti. He also filled notebooks of several sizes. Not all those notes made it into his computer files or reports. Art still preferred pen and paper. Sometimes even pencil and paper, which made for eye strain. The result was slow going for Matthew, who had to start by sorting out which note went with which investigation and in what order.

It didn't take him long to discover that his fellow detective had been digging into the histories of several officers within the department, including the two he'd mentioned to Matthew. His interest hadn't started with them, though; apparently, he'd already become uneasy, pursuing what Matthew guessed were several of the same threads as Alexa's.

What had interested Art most, though, were ones who'd been caught using the services of prostitutes when they were supposed to be arresting them. He was sure one had given warnings a couple of times right before operations, meaning the run-down motels that were supposed to be the hot spots had proved astonishingly peaceful and crime-free when the cops showed up to hammer on doors.

Sergeant Newsome called Peters on it, Art had noted. Matthew had to squint to read his handwriting. *Peters admitting having a relationship with*—this name was illegible—*and he's afraid he let the plans slip. Says he's not seeing her anymore. Knows it was stupid (ya think???), groveled. Newsome chewed him out and let it go with a warning.*

Matthew sat back to mull over the incident. Was Vice sergeant Newsome really that naïve? Did he have complete faith in his officers? As Art had probably done, Matthew grunted in disbelief.

What Art was looking for, it appeared, was any connection between the cops who'd gotten too friendly with hookers and the murders of several of the local ones.

Stunned by where this trail seemed to be heading, Matthew found himself queasily agreeing with the logic. No arrests had been made for a reason; the pimps that might otherwise be suspected had unshakable alibis, and witnesses were either nonexistent or too intimidated to come forward. What's more, the killings had looked damned cold-blooded, not displaying the kind of rage they'd see if a john had lost it.

A man threatened with the possibility of losing his job now, especially a man who routinely carried a gun and had a good idea how to avoid leaving any trace of his presence at a crime scene... Yeah, that made sense.

Matthew blew out an unhappy breath. Then he went back to sifting through notes that were too often nonsensical, in hope of finding the open spots in the puzzle where they belonged.

INVITING LIEUTENANT MATTHEW REINERT to dinner a second night, and in a row, wasn't the smartest thing Alexa had ever done. She and her voice of common sense needed to talk before she got too carried away. As in, asking him to stay the night.

Just say no.

She wrinkled her nose. The fact that she was worrying at all about whether she'd do that meant she was seriously considering it.

The doorbell rang in the middle of her attempt to squelch any enthusiasm for having sex with a man she hardly knew, one who'd rushed to her rescue, sure, but also represented a police department riddled with corruption. She wasn't yet ready to forget that.

Besides, she had some serious doubts about why *he* was interested in her. Journalist? Cop? Not exactly an obvious pairing.

When she let him in, her heart took a little hop despite everything. When he wasn't right in front of her, she forgot the impact his sheer physical presence had on her. His height, breadth, all those muscles that she felt sure weren't cultivated for show, never mind the glint in his steely eyes and the quirk of his mouth, definitely pushed her buttons.

"Smells good," he said.

"What?" She backed up. "Oh, I'm stir-frying. Ginger beef. I don't eat much meat, but I love this recipe."

He followed her toward the kitchen. "When Nate lived with me, I did a lot of stir-fries, too. I made more effort when I wasn't cooking just for myself."

Having plugged in the wok, she really studied him. Deeper than usual lines scored his face, aging him. "You look..." Alexa hesitated.

Matthew grimaced. "Lousy day."

"Detective Dwyer?" The police chief had held a press conference, looking outraged and determined. She'd wondered how much was sincere.

"No change in Art's condition." He leaned a hip against the edge of the countertop. "Is there anything I can do?"

"Give the rice a quick stir?"

He complied. "Art's wife is going through hell. Telling her was—" He rubbed his forehead with the back of his hand.

Art Dwyer had been with the local department for fifteen years, Alexa now knew, having started his career with a few years in Portland, Oregon. He had to be older than Matthew, who outranked him, but not everyone wanted to take on administrative responsibilities. Truthfully, she was surprised that Matthew did. Or maybe she shouldn't be; he did have what seemed like an effortless air of command. Probably, he couldn't help himself.

Dumping strips of beef into the sizzling oil to join the green onions and ginger that smelled so good, she said, "There's no way to ease into it, is there? Being the one to deliver the news…" She shivered. That would be bad enough, but loving the man who lay in a coma because someone had tried to *kill* him—*that* would be worse. The fact that she could so easily imagine being in that position scared her.

He lifted the lid of the pan on the stovetop. "I think the rice is done."

Think about this later, Alexa warned herself.

"Set it aside and put that other pan on the burner. Asparagus," she told him.

They kept talking. Matthew gradually worked the subject back to his friend and the friend's family. Alexa winced. One kid in his first year of college, the other a sophomore in high school. If their father died, neither was at a good age to be hit with such a hammer blow—although, really, was there such a thing as a good age? Babies, toddlers, wouldn't feel the devastation, but then they'd be fated to grow up with no memory of their father, which was hard in a different way.

He asked about her family, not her favorite subject, but he'd said enough about his own, she answered.

"No father. I love my mother, and I know she loves me, but she absolutely refused to talk about him. If she'd gone the sperm bank route, wouldn't you think she'd have said?" Alexa shrugged, as if lacking any knowledge at all of her father wasn't still as sore to the touch as the worst bruise. "I can't imagine her sleeping around to the point she didn't know which man was the father when she got pregnant. It was a shock having her marry when I was eight, but that only lasted a few years."

Matthew watched her with interest. "She's still alive?"

"Oh, sure, and as stubborn as ever." Alexa grimaced. "When I was a teenager, I descended so far as to search her closet and the boxes stashed in the attic for evidence. How could there not be something?"

"Is she still in the house where you grew up?"

"Yep. My grandparents gave her a great deal on it when they retired to Florida, which means Mom *also* grew up in that house."

"You picture yourself moving back there when she's gone?"

She gave a slight shrug. "I really don't think so. It's hard enough to separate myself from Mom's stern voice. If she were a ghost and I were living there, she'd never quit lecturing me."

Matthew laughed. "So does this big mystery in your life explain why you've been hunting for answers to other questions ever since?"

She grimaced. "Probably?"

That earned her another laugh.

He looked so tired, once they finished their meal she refused his help cleaning up, letting him relax over a cup of coffee. Not until she'd closed the dishwasher and joined him again at the table did she say,

"Did this happen when your friend was looking for Berkey?" She felt selfish, but almost hoped not; that the shooting had nothing to do with her problems.

Creases deepened on Matthew's forehead. He moved his shoulders as if to release tension. "I'm asking you not to put this in print. But… Art and a detective from the county sheriff's office went to what turned out to be a vacant house because Jim Berkey was supposedly squatting there."

"His name was used *again* to set someone up, only this time it was Detective Dwyer?"

"Yes. Except Berkey's name has been bandied around enough lately, every scumbag in town may have known that Art was hunting for the guy. Cops make enemies. He had a lot of open investigations."

"But…" Yet again, Alexa found herself deeply disturbed for reasons she didn't understand. Because this man could, despite his air of confidence and solid competence, as easily be a target? Could have *been* a target?

"What if you'd gone instead?" she rushed to say.

His face closed, but the hand that lay on the table fisted. She expected him to shrug her off but, after a moment, he said, "I almost did."

"Then you—" Even the possibility stole her breath.

"I didn't." He reached for her hand.

She squeezed it back and held on tight.

"I'd asked Art—" his voice was hoarse "—to find Berkey. He was the public face of the investigation. I think that bullet had his name on it."

And Matthew felt guilty, she realized.

"You assign investigations. That's what you do. It could have been any detective during any investigation."

Emotion flickered through his gray eyes, darker than usual, but eventually he nodded. "You're right. But, you know, patrol officers are killed more often than detectives. It's not something that I usually worry about."

She nodded.

"I want to believe Art will wake up anytime. He started to tell me something right before he left, but—" He clamped his lips shut.

She opened her mouth to ask him what that was, but stopped herself. "I'm being nosy, aren't I? You have no reason to tell me all. Especially given that I'm a journalist."

"No, I can't tell you everything. I do want to remind you to keep being careful." Now he sounded grimmer than she liked.

"As if I'd forgotten," she mumbled. "I will, but..."

He raised dark eyebrows.

"Given what I do for a living, I'm kind of used to acquiring enemies. Cops aren't the only ones that happens to."

"No." He sighed, swallowed the last of what had to be cold coffee by now, and said, "I'd better get out of here."

"You look exhausted." Worried, too, but she didn't say that.

When he pushed back his chair, she rose to walk him to the front door. He wouldn't be asking to stay, she could tell, which was both a relief and…a slight letdown.

This was not the right time for anything like that, she told herself firmly. She still had plenty of questions about why he was here at all, anyway. He could be visiting her conspicuously to make a statement. *Don't mess with her. I'm watching.* Or maybe he was playing good cop to soften her antagonism toward the department and city.

Only, she knew that whatever his underlying motivation, he was physically attracted to her. That would be hard to fake.

At the front door, he stopped short of reaching for the knob.

"Alexa." Just that. He held out a hand.

She hesitated, but couldn't resist so much temptation and laid her hand in his. He drew her to him, and she went. When he first bent to her height, he gently bumped his forehead against hers and nuzzled her. Only then did he seek her mouth.

The electricity was immediate. There was none of the usual awkwardness. He explored and tempted instead of demanded, and by the time he stroked his tongue along the seam of her lips, she was already parting them. He tasted of dinner and coffee and something indefinable. *Him*, she thought hazily. By this time, she'd risen on tiptoe and flung one arm around his neck while her other hand gripped his shirt as if to make sure he couldn't get away.

He pulled her in tight to his big, solid body. And, oh, it was all she could do not to rub herself against him, but she had that much self-control. She kneaded his neck, though, and savored that thigh-to-chest contact—and the evidence that he definitely did want her.

Matthew was the one to gentle the kiss, nibble on her lower lip and then her earlobe, go back to nuzzling before finally sighing. One of his hands gripped a hip, half lifting her, while the other cupped the back of her head. All ten fingers flexed before he deliberately released her. Alexa was slower to follow suit.

She blinked a few times before seeing his wry expression.

"I hope we can...take this up another time," he said in a voice that was a little rougher than usual.

"I... I hadn't—" She stopped short of an outright lie.

Now he looked sardonic. "This can't be a surprise to you."

"No." She made a face at him.

He smiled crookedly. "Good night, Alexa." Once he'd opened the door, he pressed another brief kiss on her lips, said, "Lock up tight," and loped toward his big pickup.

She did flip the dead bolt and then all but collapsed against the door.

THE NEXT DAY, Alexa stepped into warmth, the good smell of grilled burgers and deep-fat-fried potatoes, the clatter of cutlery on dishes and the voices of diners chatting while they ate. The man who'd reluctantly agreed to talk to her had chosen this out-of-the-way diner, presumably in the hope none of his fellow cops would see them together.

"I'm meeting someone here," she told the hostess, and scanned the booths that ran around the outside of the dining room. She was sure he'd prefer a booth to a more open table or the stools at the counter. In fact… "Oh, I think that's him."

In his forties, Scott Travers was still a uniformed patrol officer. A thin man whose hair was receding, his eyes never left her as she walked the length of the room to the back corner booth. When she reached it, she said, "Officer Travers?"

He flicked a glance toward the nearest table and she realized her mistake. He was out of uniform today and didn't want to be identified as a cop. But all he said was, "Scott."

She nodded and slid in to face him. "Alexa."

"Yeah, I met you just to ask—" He broke off at the appearance of a waitress.

Both ordered, Alexa having barely glanced at the menu. She might as well squeeze in lunch, however high fat. She did love cheeseburgers and fries.

Only when they were alone again did she say, "Ask me what?"

"I don't want to be in the newspaper." He sounded desperate. "I don't know how you found out about the one thing—"

"I have my own confidential informants."

He swore and let his head fall.

Their drinks arrived, giving him a reprieve. After

a sip of her soda, she said, "I won't make a promise until I hear your side."

The word that escaped him sounded more despairing than angry, which was an improvement on most of her interactions with the cops on her list.

Scott Travers was the first to agree to sit down with her. Her calls hadn't otherwise gotten her far, most recipients cutting her off before she even had the chance to give her spiel—the one about how she was open to all sides in any contentious situation, that she wasn't trying to trap anyone into incriminating himself. No "herself," as she'd told Matthew, since every cop on her list was male.

Of course, that might have to do with how few women deputies and officers served in this eastern Washington county outside Spokane.

Alexa had expected to batter her head against the blue wall of silence that famously prevented law enforcement officers from condemning each other's mistakes, crimes or misconduct. What disturbed her was her certainty that many officers weren't refusing to talk to her out of any deep loyalty to the fraternity. Nope, they were running scared.

She was still tempted to pop into one of the city's three precincts this afternoon and go face-to-face with her targets, but that wasn't compatible with being careful, per Matthew's advice. As it was, she had taken a circuitous route on quiet residential streets to get here.

Still, she couldn't let herself surrender to nerves. Especially not since the brief flurry of records released to her had passed, just like unexpected snow that wasn't sticking. The two law enforcement agencies as well as city and county governments were digging in their heels.

"Will you tell me why you accepted a bribe?" she asked, seeing no reason to whitewash the choice he'd made.

His throat worked. His gaze fastened on her again. "I was getting slammed. My ex kept needing money beyond childcare for our boy. He's really smart, being offered chances at special summer programs. One at the UW. She's working, too, but in an office. I just… I should have said no, but how could I?"

Call her skeptical but… "These drug traffickers just happened to know the right moment to hit you up?"

He heaved a sigh. "No. I pulled this guy over. Ran him, figured out who he worked for, and had reason to make him pop his trunk. He was transporting a load of coke. I'd taken him out of the car and was starting to cuff him when he said if I let him go, he could do something for me. I hate drugs!" He swallowed again. "But—"

"The temptation was too great."

He swallowed. "I guess so."

"Nobody in the department ever found out?"

Travers shook his head. "As far as I know. I claimed the license plate I gave when I first called in the stop was wrong."

"And then falsified your report."

The desperation seeped from him like the stink

when someone ate too much garlic. She was afraid he was about to cry. But what if he was playing her? "I don't even know how you found out."

Nor would she tell him. She especially wouldn't tell him that all *she'd* known was that he'd been seen accepting a packet in a surreptitious manner, and that by "a citizen" hoping she'd look into it. She'd gone with her best guess and hit a bull's-eye.

"Have they approached you again?" she asked.

"Sure. They've threatened to rat on me, but I told them I wasn't going to help. If I lose my job, so be it. That's been... I don't know, seven or eight months? Nothing's happened."

The waitress showed up to put their meals in front of them, and neither said anything until she'd bustled away. Picking up a french fry, Alexa asked then, "And your son attended the summer program at UW?"

"Yeah." Pride flashed on his face. He reached behind him for his wallet and flipped it open, finding a photo and pushing it in front of her. "That's him, getting the certificate."

The resemblance was clear between the thin, gawky boy and his father. The kid was grinning in the picture.

"He's a senior now. He applied to Stanford and got their early acceptance. We're hoping for a good financial aid offer. They seem to really want him."

Alexa opened her mouth to ask what he'd do if that offer didn't measure up, but he kept talking.

"He'll be applying to the University of Washington, too, and even Eastern, just in case. He knows we're not loaded."

She smiled and pushed the wallet back across the table.

They ate, talking generalities at first then about the department. He was more open than she had expected, not willing to name names, but acknowledging some of the issues she was investigating.

Alexa quirked her eyebrow. "Taking bribes to allow criminal acts to pass unnoticed is another category altogether, though."

Alarm flashed. "I'd never do it again!"

"I...actually believe you," she said slowly. "Me, I'm after the officers who take payoffs on a regular basis. Who work hand-in-hand with drug traffickers, say, or maybe a pimp. And the ones with a history of excessive use of force."

He pushed his empty plate away. "You know, most of us hope you scare the department into doing some housecleaning. That doesn't mean I can afford to help you."

Sad that individual cops all had to be afraid of what would happen to them, or even to their families, if they spoke out openly about the bad apples they had to work with.

She assured Scott Travers, who'd at least had the guts to meet with her, that unless she learned he'd lied to her, his name wouldn't appear in print. Her instinct said he was a good cop who'd stumbled only the once.

Unfortunately, her investigation into his more corrupt coworkers was going nowhere despite the pressure Diana was applying. She kept getting told the same old lines. Alexa wasn't the only individual making requests. Budget cuts meant the public records personnel were dealing with a backlog of a thousand or more requests. They were working as fast as they could, but individuals like her who insisted on making multiple requests even in a single day weren't helping.

A thousand requests? Really? Alexa would believe it of a city the size of Seattle or even Portland. Maybe. The city of Wilden employed a hundred and fifty officers, though, the county less than a hundred. Were that many members of the public demanding records from that police department? Not a chance. And no, the county in the form of the sheriff's office wasn't showing any more willingness to cooperate.

Of course she had other investigations ongoing, but backing off wasn't in her nature. She wasn't about to buckle to the campaign of terror. All it told her was that somebody was desperate to prevent her from zeroing in on his record, and that couldn't be because he'd accepted a few bribes or used his access to information for personal reasons.

No, the man who was so determined to stall her, if not eliminate her altogether, was hiding something that would cost him his job at the very least, and probably put him away in the state correctional institute. *He* was afraid she was too good at her job.

That meant her focus had to have turned his way, however glancingly.

Now, she had to figure out when and how.

And was he one of the men she'd called today?

Chapter Ten

Still immersed in Art Dwyer's records that afternoon, Matthew would have preferred not to take a call from Dispatch, but assigning detectives was part of his job. Damn it, he'd barely gotten off the phone with Michelle only to learn that there'd been no change in Art's condition.

"Reinert here," he said, recognizing the woman's voice.

"The manager of the solid waste transfer station says a garbage truck just dumped a body. They've stopped the machinery and kept the driver from leaving. I've dispatched an officer, but assume you'll want a detective there as soon as possible."

"I will." He jotted down names and additional information, thanked her, and ended the call. Kurt Gannon was next up in the rotation, followed by Bonnie Mendoza. Instead of picking up his phone again, he stood and looked out at the bullpen. Both detectives were working at their desks. Kurt could have handled this alone…but Bonnie could still use some seasoning.

He called them into his office, gave them what

he had and sent them on their way. "Let me know as soon as you have an ID."

Kurt, nearing retirement, was the "one foot in front of the other" kind of guy—no intuitive leaps there—but he knew how to do the job. Bonnie, barely thirty, had impressed Matthew, although she didn't have quite a year as a detective under her belt.

He tried to put the death they were investigating out of his mind, but he knew why he couldn't. The most recent murder he'd worked himself—along with Art Dwyer—was the prostitute whose body had been found in a garbage container. People rarely climbed into a dumpster on their own to die. This latest victim was male, though, so they weren't looking at another prostitute.

His distraction didn't keep him from flipping open yet another notebook and seeing the date at the top of the first page: the morning of the day Art had been gunned down. Chilled, he started reading.

Art had gone back the previous night to talk to all the girls working the part of town where Tansy Gould's body had been found. He'd met with more uneasiness, more headshakes, but he'd handed out cards again and, come morning, had received a call.

Kept her voice low so no one could overhear her, he'd written, *but she says she's not the only one who saw Tansy get in the pickup truck. Didn't see her again. Word is a cop was one of her regulars. She was scared to say no even though he didn't pay, and Johnny wouldn't have let her anyway. Amber is sure that was the cop. Of course, none of them saw the li-*

cense plate. The nib of Art's pen had dug deep into the lined paper on that last sentence. He knew the women were observant enough to be able to identify a regular who frightened one of them.

A cop.

That's what Art had wanted to talk about before the interruption that day. Not just about dirty cops, but about the likelihood one of them was also killing women he didn't trust to keep their mouths shut.

Or maybe just because he enjoyed killing. He could do so almost at will given how vulnerable these particular victims had been.

Matthew flipped back through the pages he'd separated out where Art had speculated on who in the department might be capable of being a monster even as he carried a badge.

Half a dozen names jumped out at Matthew. He knew all of the men.

Don Rommel. Mike Swartz. Rick Shanahan. Ken Kasperson. Brian Danner. John Blykowski.

Seeing Kasperson's name in this context surprised Matthew. Blykowski was a sheriff's deputy, and their paths had barely passed. The other four, he'd never liked.

Art had a B list, too, that included Jim Ward, one of the two cops he'd overheard talking about the brutal traffic stop. Wonder of wonders, both Ward and O'Brien had been fired yesterday. From what Matthew heard, even the union reps hadn't fought the decision hard. What Matthew suspected was that the chief knew Alexa was watching and had deluded himself that this might head her off.

Now, he scrabbled for his own notes, where he'd written down additional names of officers who'd done something that caught Art's attention. The six, though, were the ones Art knew or suspected had been caught at one time or another because they'd gotten involved with a prostitute or compelled one to service him. It happened. Matthew read about officers in other cities arrested because they ran an escort service on the side or were in the employ of the owner of a topless bar whose girls were available for additional hire.

There were some real pieces of scum out there, but Matthew hadn't wanted to believe Wilden PD harbored anyone that crooked.

Speaking of delusion, he thought ruefully. Art had had good instincts, and he wasn't making any bones about his belief that a cop was the killer they were looking for.

Come to think of it, Art and Alexa would have had a lot to talk about if they'd had the chance to sit down together. *Please, God, they did have that chance.*

Question was how many of the names Art had highlighted were also on Alexa's list?

A visit to the records department was one way of getting answers. She'd have requested camera footage or reports on particular incidents, but he had no doubt she'd also sought discipline records for a number of individual officers.

His phone rang, Kurt Gannon's name popping up.

"No ID on the guy," the detective said, "and he looks like he might have been living on the street. Skin and teeth, you know how it is."

Matthew knew.

"Thing is, Bonnie recognized him from when she was in uniform. Called himself Jim Berkey. Supposedly gave us occasional tips." That last was wary; Gannon had heard the rumors.

"Not all good ones," Matthew said grimly. "He originated that debacle involving Alexa Adams. His name was used to lure Art to the location where he was shot, too."

"It wasn't Berkey who set up Art. He was already dead. The medical examiner isn't here yet, but I'd say two or three days, tops."

"He almost has to have been in hiding." If the CI had had any brains left at all, he'd have started wondering if whoever talked him into passing on false information might be afraid that under pressure Berkey'd give up the name.

"Keep me informed," Matthew told his detective and ended the call.

This murder cemented his fear that Alexa was indeed at the center of a lot of unsettling events. She was just as much a threat to a killer cop as Art had been—before he'd been gunned down.

Matthew frowned into space. He wanted to put an around-the-clock bodyguard on her. No, he wanted to *be* her around-the-clock bodyguard, but he couldn't imagine she'd agree to that. After all, the woman was investigating multiple officers in this department.

How was she supposed to do that if the lieutenant in charge of the major crimes division was watching everything she did and eavesdropping on every conversation?

And just who *had* she talked to? he wondered.

Better question: if he was open with her about his suspicions, was there any chance at all that she'd share and share alike?

Uh-uh. Why did he feel sure trust didn't come easily to Alexa Adams?

SHE *REALLY* HAD to learn to say no.

The only good reason to encourage Matthew Reinert to hang around was if she believed for even a teeny, tiny second that he could be coaxed into an indiscretion about his fellow officers.

Alexa scrunched up her nose. That was extremely unlikely, and not true anyway. He'd come rushing to rescue her when she called. That was worth something. Still, when he'd called offering to bring a pizza, she could have said, "Oh, gosh, I have plans. Can we do that another night?"

But no. She'd hesitated, credit to her first healthy instinct for self-preservation, then succumbed without listening to the inner voice saying, *Whoa! Think about this*.

So now she was listening for the sound of his deep-throated truck in her driveway, to be followed by a doorbell or firm knock on the door *he'd* installed for her.

Why hadn't she realized how sneaky his generous effort had been?

And there was the engine, quickly cut off, followed by the doorbell.

She was dumb enough to feel anticipation lurking beneath all the common sense warnings she'd been giving herself.

Letting him in, she said, "This isn't a good idea. Why are you here?"

He smiled, kissed her lightly and said, "Why else?"

"I can think of a bunch of underhanded reasons," she mumbled to his back as she locked up before trailing him to the kitchen.

He surveyed the table, where she'd already set out two placemats, napkins, plates and a beer for him and a rare glass of wine for her. If there was a glint of amusement in his eyes when he glanced at her, she could hardly blame him.

Not until they sat down did she get a good look at his face. Oh, he might have been smiling, but tonight that was just surface. Lines too deep, eyes too dark, tension changing the set of his shoulders.

"Your friend?" Surely, she'd have heard if Art Dwyer had died, but— It could have just happened.

"No change. I stopped by the hospital on my way here."

"Oh." She plopped down in her chair. This had to be getting to him. "There's nothing else wrong?"

He sighed and sat, too, placing the pizza box in the middle of the table and opening it. "I have some worries," he admitted. "But can we eat before we talk about it?"

"*I'll* just worry."

He muttered something, dished up a couple of slices of the pizza and pushed the box closer to her. "Yeah, okay."

She took a slice, but didn't start eating.

"Jim Berkey? His body was found today."

She absorbed that. "Oh. You said you hadn't been able to find him."

"He wasn't dead the whole while, but someone got to him before we did." The dark undertone was unmistakable.

"You think…" Alexa hesitated.

"I do think."

Once again, he'd managed to scare her.

Matthew started to eat, making her realize he really was hungry. She wasn't so much, after her greasy lunchtime indulgence. She nibbled, though, watching him devour half the large pizza with the kind of mechanical hunger that made her wonder if he was even tasting his food.

Finally, he sighed and met her eyes. "Can we talk off the record?"

The last time he'd asked that same question, she'd almost laughed at him. Now…a shocking amount had changed.

ALEXA'S EYES NARROWED.

Talking to her about an open investigation shouldn't be an option, even if she hadn't been a journalist. But, damn it, she was in the middle of every problem on his desk, and Matthew didn't think that was by chance. She might as well have had a bull's-eye painted on her front door. No, Matthew thought immediately, make that right in the middle of her back, and that's what scared him. What if he had to sit at her side in the cubicle next to Art's, praying for a flicker of her eyelashes?

When Jackman had pulled her car over and found out it came tagged with an "armed and dangerous" designation, they were all lucky that simple traffic stop hadn't turned into a tragedy. Alexa had done the logical thing in pulling her registration out of the glove box; under the circumstances, any cop would have been jumpy enough to wonder what she was really going for.

Matthew had no doubt that her focused investigation into problem officers was the reason both incidents had happened, just as Art's similar investigation provided the motive for his attempted murder. That meant, if she wouldn't step out on the limb, he just about had to.

"I hope you'll keep this to yourself, but I think I have to tell you. Art Dwyer had come up with a list of rotten cops," he said bluntly. "With my attention pulled too many ways, he's been the primary looking into the killing of a prostitute whose body was found shortly after the raid on your house. Not the first one killed, either, as you probably know. He came to me to talk about what he suspected, but we were interrupted. He was in a coma before we could finish that conversation."

"I read about it. But...you're saying..." Her mouth opened, closed, opened again. "That you believe he was shot by a fellow *cop*?" Her voice had risen toward the end. "Maybe the same one—"

He said stiffly, "I have to consider it a real possibility now that I've had time to dig through his notes."

Even as she still stared in apparent shock, he saw that she'd started thinking. "But...why me?" Alexa shook her head. "Dumb question. I already know the answer. He has to be someone whose background I'm digging into. We'd already guessed as much. Did he not know Detective Dwyer was asking the same questions?"

"Maybe not, initially. But at some point, he found out. That's why I'm hoping to compare notes. There may be a lot of commonality between your list and Art's, but there might not be, too."

"If there are only a couple of officers he and I were both investigating..."

Matthew bent his head. "I'd have a really good place to start."

They stared at each other until his eyes burned and he had to blink first.

"I can't reveal sources. You know that," Alexa almost whispered.

"I'm not asking for sources. Only for a list of who you're investigating. I shouldn't be telling you any of this," he said roughly, "but if what I'm suspecting is true, this son of a bitch has already killed several women and tried to kill a good cop to protect his secrets. He won't hesitate to go after you again."

Thus the creepy-crawly feeling she had every time she stepped out her front door lately, even if she was only walking out to the street to get her mail or newspaper. Art Dwyer hadn't been gunned down on his own porch, but from the killer's point of view, why not repeat something that had worked so well the first time?

She shivered just thinking that.

"My editor—oh, and the executive editor—would fire me if they knew I was even *thinking* of cooperating with you."

"Packing up and taking a leave of absence right now would be smart," Matthew said, those sharp gray eyes drilling into her. "That would be a good alternative to cooperating with my investigation."

"He—whoever he is—would have to know I could keep looking for answers long distance. What if he sets out to find me? And…what? Do I disappear for a week? Two weeks? Months?"

Matthew didn't know what to tell her. He could dig deeper into the reasons Art had put each man on his list, but what were the odds he'd be able to actually place one of them in the alley behind the vacant house at the right time? Hell, that would take a miracle.

Crinkles between her eyebrows let him know she was holding a serious internal debate.

He held his breath, awaiting the outcome.

Finally, Alexa huffed, her eyes drawn to his. "Can I see your list, instead of the other way around?"

"Will you promise me that you won't start an investigation on anyone I name unless you stumble across information on your own?"

Indignation had her gaping at him. "How can I not—" She mumbled a few words under her breath. "Fine. I won't forget those names, though."

He suppressed a smile. "I wouldn't expect you to."

"Let me put the pizza in the fridge before we start. Unless you want more?"

"No, I'm done." He started to rise. "I can do that—"

"That's okay." She already had the box closed. "Don't forget it when you go. I can't imagine I'd eat much of it, and what's left would probably be barely enough for your lunch tomorrow."

He'd relaxed enough to laugh. "You're right."

A moment later, they settled down again, him cracking open a second beer. He had a written list folded in his pocket, but those six names that had lit up like neon signs, he knew without refreshing his memory. He was reluctant to include the two that had surprised him—especially Kasperson, who seemed like an okay guy—but he needed to find out whether she knew anything about them, too.

"John Blykowski."

Alexa blinked a couple of times. "Sheriff's deputy."

"Yeah."

"I'm looking into his background. He's not at the top of my list, but I heard something about him."

Matthew gave a clipped nod. "Ken Kasperson."

"Never heard of him."

But she was tucking that name into a safe place for future reference, he felt sure.

"Don Rommel."

"Oh yeah."

Ditto for the last three names. Her lip curled at two of the names: Brian Danner and Rick Shanahan.

"Can you tell me what you've heard about these men?"

She had to mull it over some more before she decided to answer his question.

"Their involvement with hookers," she said finally. "All of them, except the guy I'd never heard of."

Matthew scraped a hand over his face. "That's why they interested Art, too. What I don't know is whether he'd learned anything to make him think one of them had committed acts of violence toward the women to protect his reputation and job."

"Versus just breaking the law and even keeping it from being enforced?"

"Yeah," he said with new weariness. He didn't mention two other possibilities: that the list should be longer, cops who'd committed the same infractions not having been caught yet, and that the officer inciting the assaults on Alexa was one she was investigating for behavior that had nothing to do with hookers.

Then Alexa really did shock him.

Chapter Eleven

"You remember the cop who was killed two years ago?" she asked, sounding unusually tentative.

That was enough to make him stiffen.

No, he hadn't forgotten the first law enforcement officer killed in the line of duty in this county in fifty-two years. If Art didn't survive, he'd be the second. Matthew swore. "Do you have any reason to believe there's a connection?"

Alexa squirmed a little. "He wanted to talk to me. Said he'd gone to his commanding officer and been told, in essence, to shut his mouth. I agreed to see him, but he dragged his feet." She shrugged. "I think he had mixed feelings about talking to a journalist. He was killed before we could set up a meeting."

"I had no idea. What did you do?"

"I talked to his wife, just tiptoeing around, you know, but I didn't get any vibe that he'd told her about what he'd seen on the job that was disturbing enough he'd take it to an outsider. Especially a journalist. He was proud to wear the badge, she'd said. I called a few of his friends for statements." Her mouth twisted. "His commanding officer, too."

"I remember the article," he said slowly. "You didn't even hint. I wondered about it, though, mostly because your name doesn't usually appear on straightforward news items."

"It got assigned to me because he'd wanted to tell me something. I did what digging I could, but got no-where. Now I can't help wishing…"

He couldn't help doing the same. He'd try to keep it quiet, but Matthew had every intention of finding out what patrol officer Alan Sharpe had done in the weeks immediately preceding his death.

"There was an intense investigation, of course," he said, "but the detectives came up empty. We all make enemies over the course of our careers, so there were too many places to look."

She nodded. "So, now what?"

Without being really specific, he told her what he intended, and she didn't question his vagueness. He'd already given her more than he should have, and she knew it. If Chief Paulson learned about this conver-sation, Matthew's head would roll.

Face it, having a relationship with a journalist wouldn't be easy. They'd be dodging land mines constantly.

What did you do at work today, dear?

Uh, sorry, I can't tell you.

And yet, Matthew tried not to lie to himself. He wanted Alexa Adams, prickly as she could be. He liked her brains, her courage, and the empathy that had driven her to do what she did for a living. He liked the occasional vulnerability she'd let him see, and the knowledge that her pride refused to let her make a habit of that.

In fact, he felt way more for a woman he'd known for only a week than he should.

Damn, he didn't want to go, but she was the one who had to do the asking before he could stay, and he suspected the idea hadn't even crossed her mind this evening. She'd be as eager to start her research as he was, given new strings to pull.

When he pushed back his chair, she did look surprised but glanced at the clock. "I didn't realize it was getting so late."

Eight o'clock.

"Pizza," she reminded him and then walked him to the door as she did every time he came over.

This time, he didn't reach for the knob. Instead, he stood gazing down at her face, seeing so many shifting emotions and thoughts, he couldn't read any of them. She didn't retreat from him, though, and when he set down the pizza box on the chest by the door and slipped a hand around the back of her neck, she lifted her own hand to rest it on his chest.

Her voice soft, husky, she murmured, "Good night."

Matthew made some sound in his throat, definitely nonverbal, and bent his head. Tonight, he aimed for gentle. He had to build trust. Something about the quiver of her lips, the way her pupils contracted, the bite of her fingers when they flexed on his pectoral muscle, challenged his determination. When his tongue slid into her mouth, the tastes were as complex as she was. He wanted more.

She rose on tiptoe, fists closed on his shirt as he deepened the kiss and gripped her taut butt to lift her. Twice he had to pull back so they could both breathe; twice, he dove back in for more.

But, damn, he knew better. She responded to him with all the heat he could hope for, but that wasn't the same as her inviting him into her bed when she was in her right mind. The last thing he wanted was her to regret their love making.

So, finally, he lifted his head, said in an unrecognizable voice, "I need to go," and waited for her to blink repeatedly until her brain kicked into gear.

When she dropped back to her heels, nodded and released his shirt, Matthew wasn't surprised. He couldn't deny disappointment; he was so aroused, the idea of going home and booting up his laptop to browse what records he could access was unimaginable.

As was getting a good night's sleep.

He kissed her again, lightly, grabbed the pizza and said, "Good night." Alexa behind him, he opened the door, scanned the front yard and stepped out onto the porch.

"I'm sorry."

He turned back, his smile rueful. "I understand, you know. We're not an obvious pair, are we?"

An answering tremulous smile made his heart give an odd thump.

"I don't know about that. I'm beginning to think—" Her eyes widened as she cut that thought off.

He'd already been hit by how much they had in common. Still, this was too soon. He wasn't even a hundred percent sure *he* could trust her not to run with what he'd told her tonight.

"We have time," he told her. "In the meantime, you be careful."

"And once again, we end an evening on an upbeat note."

Descending the porch steps, he was amused by her effort to convince him that she could take care of herself, thank you very much. At the same time…her gutsy attitude scared him. So much so that when he slid in behind the wheel of his pickup, he gave serious thought to circling the block and coming back to park where he could see her house and watch over her.

But a direct attack… No, that seemed unlikely after the elaborate efforts to get to her using other members of the police department. He expected more of the same. But when and how?

"I THINK I need to quit threatening and actually file a suit," Alexa's attorney announced the next morning. "All this foot-dragging and the excuses are starting to really tick me off."

Alexa put her phone on speaker and poured herself her second cup of coffee for the morning. "Really? It took you this long?"

Diana laughed. "You've had longer to work up a temper."

"Oh, come on! You must deal with government officials all the time."

"True." She sighed. "Okay, anything new I need to know?"

"No. I really want to interview these guys, but I don't have enough ammunition to apply serious pressure until I see the information in the records I've requested. Catch-22."

"No new releases?"

"No. After that little spurt of not very interesting stuff, I'm getting a resounding lack of action."

"So what *are* you doing?"

"Oh, mostly working from home. Finishing up another series, pursuing what leads I can with this one. You know, calling victims."

"Who give you an earful."

"Yep. It's really maddening when I *know* there's body or squad car camera footage that will give me a lot better idea what really happened."

"Will the newspaper help us lean on the city?"

"Oh, they've already put some weight behind my requests, but we hadn't quite reached the point of filing suit when all this intimidation started happening. I know they'll join us in a suit, and probably foot the bill. In fact, let me give you the name of the head of their legal department."

Turned out that Diana already knew who that was. She promised to call then asked, "What about your cop?"

"*My* cop?"

Diana snorted.

"He's still holding back some things. I guess he has to," Alexa said grudgingly. "I think more stuff has been happening that links back to me than the department is willing to admit."

"What about the detective who was just shot?"

Alexa didn't say a word. The silence spoke for itself.

Her attorney said crisply, "I assume your car plates are up to date, the sticker hasn't happened to fall off, and you're driving like a little old lady. You don't even *think* about rolling through a stop sign even if there's no other car visible for blocks?"

Alexa hated to admit it, but who else could she be honest with? Well, her editor, up to a point, and Matthew. But since he wasn't a hundred percent up-front with her, she was left in an emotional tangle where he was concerned.

"Um, I'm not driving any more than I can help, and then not out on busier roads where someone might spot me." She hesitated. "Lieutenant Reinert would prefer I stay on lockdown at home until he gets to the bottom of this."

The lengthy pause held a significance Alexa recognized. "You're sure he isn't impeding your investigation by pretending to be your buddy?"

"I…really think he's sincere. But I'm suspicious by nature, so naturally I've considered the possibility." Was that true? she had to ask herself. Or had her attraction to him made her foolishly credulous?

She couldn't honestly answer that question.

OFFICER ALAN SHARPE had worked a couple of prostitute stings in the weeks before his death.

Matthew sat back in his desk chair. Damn, he'd been hoping there'd be no link to the problems Art Dwyer had seen...but deluding himself never did work very well.

And yeah, Jim Ward had been dinged for "inappropriate" actions on a similar sting.

Why, Matthew couldn't help wondering, did the department waste so much time and manpower on trying to control or eliminate prostitution in their small city when all the efforts to date had achieved absolutely nothing? Except, maybe, corrupt some law enforcement officers.

He had to remind himself that whoever had killed Tansy Gould would have been using and discarding troubled young women no matter what, though. In fact, he'd have been less likely to draw attention to himself if he hadn't been forced to be part of a law enforcement action.

Thinking about the case, he called Kurt Gannon, the detective assigned to investigate Jim Berkey's murder.

"Wish I could tell you more," Gannon said. "We think we've found out where he went to ground, but people who knew he was there have no idea when he left. Or more likely, was grabbed."

"Okay. Short of a witness who saw him the few days before his death, we've probably reached a dead end."

Two hours later, Matthew was called into the chief's office. His temper stirred, but he told the PA he was on his way. Taking the stairs two at a time instead of the elevator, he wanted to believe Chief Paulson had summoned him for an update on the several threads of investigation, and particularly into the attempted murder of a long-time officer in his own department. Leaving that unsolved would be a blot on Paulson's reputation.

Unfortunately, Matthew had never much liked the chief, who was more politician than cop. Listening to him talk to the media, you'd think he had personally broken every case, rescued that choking child, thrown himself in the path of a bullet to save the life of an innocent woman. Hell, stopped traffic for the mama duck and her ducklings to cross the road.

The truth was, Matthew couldn't recall the last time Paulson had actually asked for updates on an investigation. He became irritated when, in his opinion, matters didn't move fast enough, but he'd convey his impatience through the several layers of authority that lay between him and his lieutenant leading the major crimes.

Paulson occupied the corner office on the third—top floor—of the police station. The door was open—nice, since he often claimed to have an open-door policy for the men and women who served—but really this was an outer door that led to his PA's desk and a waiting room. As usual, the door to the inner office was closed.

Matthew nodded to the woman behind the desk. "Ms. Yunker."

She smiled. "Lieutenant. The chief is anxious to talk to you. Go on in."

Paulson didn't rise from behind his desk after Matthew rapped lightly and walked in. He wore a crisp uniform, the hat set carefully on the corner of his remarkably pristine desk. Presumably, he'd been studying something on his computer monitor, or at least pretending to. Simmering anger already showed on a face that was developing jowls.

"Chief," Matthew said mildly. "You wanted to see me?"

"I did, and I'm sure you know why."

Because he'd gone to Records asking for everything they had on several officers within the department?

Apparently, the chief couldn't be bothered to ask for an update on Art's condition. Matthew certainly wasn't going to volunteer the latest from Michelle, who'd said there was increased activity behind Art's eyelids and his muscles and nerves had been jerking.

Now, he said, "I'm afraid not." Since he hadn't been told to take a seat, he remained standing in a relaxed parade stance.

Face turning red, Paulson roared, "What the hell do you think you're doing, investigating your fellow officers as if they were criminals!"

Keep your temper. "Sir, I have to follow where the evidence takes me. You know that. I've become convinced that an officer in this department has gone rogue and killed several people as well as shooting Detective Dwyer."

"I was told that there's no hit on the bullet recovered from the house wall," the chief snapped.

"That's correct." And news he'd received only that morning. It was interesting that the report had also gone to the police chief, and that he'd bothered to read it. "It didn't come from the gun of a career criminal, or we'd likely have at least a forensic hit."

Paulson snorted. "So you leaped to thinking one of your colleagues tried to kill your detective."

Matthew didn't like telling anyone what he was thinking—except, apparently, Alexa Adams, investigative reporter, he thought with chagrin. He didn't see that he had a choice now.

Still on his feet—too tense to sit even if he'd been offered the option—he laid it out. Dwyer had good reason to believe Tansy Gould had been obliging a local cop. He let some irony creep into his voice on the one word. *Obliging.* Witnesses felt sure the pickup truck she'd climbed into before vanishing belonged to that cop, one of her regulars.

Paulson shook his head. "Some hooker who was probably high tells you she last saw another hooker get into a police officer's personal vehicle, and you take that as gospel?"

Matthew ground his teeth. "Detective Dwyer was primary on this investigation, which included the deaths of at least three other women we believe worked as prostitutes. There were clear similarities in how they were killed, and in how their bodies were disposed of. Until now, there'd never been any witnesses, which suggests the other women were scared to speak out. Art had been asking questions within the department. I believe he alarmed the wrong person, who was afraid Art was closing in on him."

Before the chief could erupt again, Matthew added, "I also believe that same person is responsible for the false tip about the drug house that could have sent us astray, as well as tagging Ms. Adams's vehicle with a BOLO that resulted in a frightening traffic stop for her.

"We've also confirmed that the man who set up a supposed meeting with her so she could be snatched was a long-time confidential informant. The voices match. Who else but a cop could have managed all that? Who else would have known Detective Dwyer would jump at a possible chance to lay his hands on that CI?"

The chief's color had worsened, looking like a heart attack waiting to happen.

"That sounds like a fantasy you've cooked up! Is there one solid piece of evidence backing up any of this absurd story?"

Matthew opened his mouth but Paulson talked right over him.

"A hooker who *thinks* she saw. A CI who is a known crook. That seems to be the sum of it."

Somehow he kept his voice in control, but he started to lean forward, stopping himself with an effort from flattening his hands on this idiot's desktop.

"You are aware that the CI who gave the tip that meant to trigger a SWAT raid, and who also set her up to be assaulted, has now been found dead? His body left in a garbage dumpster, just as the prostitutes' bodies all have been? After all, it's pretty obvious he was only doing favors for someone. Someone who has it in for Ms. Adams, a journalist who also happens to be investigating a number of the same bad apples in this police department that Detective Dwyer also suspected?"

Paulson stood. "Be careful, Lieutenant. You sound as if you're in league with a reporter who has targeted this department to boost her career. I'll assume you intend to take a harder look for *solid* evidence that might lead you to the real perpetrator, or perpetrators. Even you have to see how ridiculous it is to tie Detective Dwyer's death to some pranks played on a journalist trying to dig up nonexistent dirt. I've told the head of records to deny your requests. You will not join that woman in trying to blacken our reputation. Is that clear?"

"It's clear," Matthew said stiffly. He bent his head slightly. "Sir." He had to get out of there before he told this useless sack of you-know-what exactly what he could do with himself.

And then he had to figure out how to bypass Chief Paulson's efforts to cut him off at the pass.

Chapter Twelve

When her phone rang, Alexa didn't recognize the number or the area code, but that wasn't unusual these days.

When she answered, a male voice said curtly, "This is Brian Danner. I've gotten your messages. I'll sit down with you if you can meet me at the Chatter Box in the next hour."

Wariness almost edged out excitement. "I can be there, but I'm curious why you've changed your mind about talking to me."

"You want to meet or not?"

"I do want."

Dead air.

Well, it wasn't as if she'd expected the guy to be friendly, or even considerate. Among his other problems, he had a reputation for a hot temper.

Within an hour. Did that mean he was already there, waiting for her? Alexa glanced down at herself, wrinkled her nose and hustled to her bedroom to change clothes and do something to her hair.

She yanked her ratty T-shirt over her head then

paused in front of her closet. Should she let Matthew know she was going out, and why?

No, of course not. The day she had to ask permission from anyone but her editor to do her job was the day she had to change careers.

A minute later, Alexa was backing her car out of the garage. She stopped in the driveway while she calculated the best way to get to the western edge of town. Of course, Danner wouldn't have suggested meeting her anywhere near the police station or either of the satellite precincts. She studied her GPS before deciding to ignore it except for the last few blocks, where she pretty much would have to join a major road.

Oh, how she hated the way her heart was pounding when she backed into the street and accelerated cautiously forward. She'd always operated with common sense, but that wasn't the same thing as the apprehension that dogged her nonstop these days. *I'll get past it*, she told herself while wondering whether she should have asked someone from the newspaper to accompany her. Or Diana Troxell maybe would have—for a sky-high, by-the-hour charge, but a cop afraid of losing his job for malfeasance wouldn't be frank in front of an attorney. And certainly not in front of a lieutenant in his own department.

At sudden movement in front of her, she braked sharply. A kid on a bike, not paying attention to traffic. She breathed deeply a few times, ordered herself to pay attention, and set off again.

At last, she reached the four-lane road that passed

in front of the Chatter Box. Because of railroad tracks behind it and a giant warehouse to one side, she could only turn into the parking lot from this street.

Three blocks.

She looked longingly at her phone, lying on the seat beside her.

One block later, a squad car burst from a parking lot to her right and the flashing lights came on, followed by a blast of the siren. Both terrified and mad at herself—she'd *known* this would happen—she put on a turn signal and pulled into the next lot, this time in front of a Mexican restaurant where she'd never eaten.

Within seconds, a uniformed officer appeared outside her window and yanked on the door handle. "Unlock! Unlock!" he yelled.

Shaking, she did as he asked.

He wrenched open the door. "Keep your hands on the wheel!"

Alexa hadn't even thought of moving them. Except, she could so easily reach over and pick up her phone...

The cop's gaze lowered to something on the front passenger-side floor. Suddenly, just as had happened the last time, he drew his big black gun.

"What are you—"

"Do you have a permit to carry a concealed weapon?"

" I don't own a gun at all!"

"Then why is there one not quite hidden on the floor?" He nodded past her.

Her head turned and her stomach rolled queasily.

Oh God, he was right. Only the grip showed, but that was undeniably a handgun, probably a semiautomatic like his.

She recoiled. "It's not mine. I swear it's not. Somebody planted it there!"

His grin was ugly. "Now, who would want to do something like that to you?"

Boy, that wasn't subtle. He was all but telling her he knew damn well how the gun had appeared in her car—but not in a way that anyone listening to a recording would recognize as gloating.

How was he going to explain pulling her over in the first place? Her gaze fell on the nametag above the pocket on his dark blue uniform shirt.

R. Shanahan.

No wonder he looked vaguely familiar. She'd studied photos of him. Late thirties, handsome if not for that sneer and the shaved head, bulky in the way of men who spent a lot of time lifting weights.

"Out of the car!" he commanded. She'd barely pushed the seat belt release when he hauled her out and shoved her roughly down on her face on the pavement. Grit ground into her cheek. His knee pressed the middle of her back. Déjà vu.

He started talking on his radio, but she couldn't quite make out what he was saying. Backup—she heard that.

Within an impossibly short period of time, two more police units pulled in, blocking her car, and two more officers stood over her, one also pointing his ugly handgun at her. Moments later, yet a third arrived. She couldn't see his face, only his legs.

Shanahan produced plastic cuffs. He wasn't gentle wrenching her arms behind her back to put them on.

"You planted that gun!" she cried. "This whole thing was a setup. You won't get away with it."

Rick Shanahan leaned forward until she could feel the heat of his breath on her cheek and whispered, "Sure we will."

None of them was pretending. She'd seen the smirks as they manhandled her.

"I'm entitled to a phone call."

"And you'll get one. Once you're at the station."

But first, he officially placed her under arrest and recited her rights. Meanwhile, a second officer also shackled her ankles.

Two of them lifted her. One hand groped her right breast. She tried to twist away, but the only result was the carelessness—or was it viciousness?—of how they tossed her into the back of Shanahan's car behind the prisoner partition.

The door slammed.

Alexa hadn't quite landed on the seat. They were probably pleased to make her as miserable as possible. Her lower body was there, but she was nose-down on the floor. She tried desperately to free a hand from the cuffs that bit into her wrists, but failed. With her arms behind her, she couldn't even use her elbows for leverage. Now, blood rushed to her head, and she was bitterly afraid she was crying.

She'd known better than to allow herself to be

grabbed again like this. If she hadn't let the attorney awaken her fears where Matthew was concerned, she'd have called him before she'd set off to a meeting like this. He wouldn't have had to drive her, or go in with her, just follow her until he saw her walking in.

The horrible position with the edge of the seat digging into her stomach brought bile to her throat. One pothole or speed bump and she'd be puking. If only she thought any of the cops would actually be responsible for cleaning it up, she might not have minded.

Struggling for calm, Alexa made herself picture the faces of the other officers. At least one other was familiar, too. Brian Danner, her caller. Oh, he'd wanted to meet up with her all right.

The other… No, she didn't know.

Which one had proposed setting up this ambush? He'd obviously found enthusiastic coconspirators.

They're afraid of me, she reminded herself. *She* had the power, and they hated that.

Keep thinking that.

She didn't quite throw up on the drive to the station, but it was a close call and the taste in her mouth was vile by the time Shanahan hauled her out and set her on her feet.

"This time she had a concealed weapon," he told someone. "You know damn well it was under the seat the last time she got pulled over. After Reinert jumped in to protect her—" his tone had become ugly "—nobody searched her car."

Forgetting her ankles, too, were restrained, she tried to take a step and fell hard. First—painfully—

to her knees then onto her side. None of the several uniformed cops had so much as put out a hand to stop the tumble.

One did bend over and cut the plastic cuffs off her ankles so she could be yanked to her feet once again, hustled through a heavy steel door, down a hall and into a small bare room. A holding cell.

She only had one thing to say. "I'm entitled to a phone call."

"You'll get one. Eventually."

The door closed with a substantial clunk, leaving her to shuffle, wincing from the pain in her knees, to the bench bolted to the floor and wall. She sat, hating the knowledge that her face was smeared with tears and snot, and that she couldn't wipe off either. At least the room didn't have a window. There was a camera mounted up in one corner, though, so somebody was probably still watching her. She wouldn't give them the satisfaction of showing any more discomfort than she could help.

Was humiliating her their endgame? Somehow, they'd planted that gun in her car, but they wouldn't find her fingerprints on it because she'd never touched it. Had they considered forcing her to pick it up? But how could they, if they were playing this for the benefit of their superiors? Turning off a vest camera wouldn't look good, not when she'd put in records requests on at least two of the officers. And there would have been the risk of being seen by a passerby on the road or a diner peering out the window of the restaurant.

If not, she strongly suspected that they'd have cooked up an excuse for having had to shoot and kill her.

As for the gun, likely they'd insist she had worn gloves when handling it. Any kindergartener knew to do that much. And what was that saying? Possession was nine-tenths of the law? She had indubitably been caught possessing that awful thing.

She had no way of checking the time, which crawled. Her nose wrinkled at the taste in her mouth, but then she realized the room stank, too. Bleach and probably vomit and maybe even blood.

Fortunately, anger stretched and replaced the humiliation. It gave her the strength to ignore her increasingly painful shoulder and plot how she'd see Rick Shanahan and all his buddies behind bars.

A scraping sound preceded the appearance of an unfamiliar officer, who had something in his hand. A phone. Her phone?

"I'll remove those cuffs now," he said. No sympathy there, but no hostility, either. "You can make a call. Only one."

Jaw clenched, Alexa didn't say anything, only shifted to give him space to free her from the handcuffs. Even so, a sound escaped her when her shoulders screamed after being released from the unnatural position.

The cop set the phone beside her. "Make the call." He crossed his arms and stayed where he was.

It wasn't easy picking up the phone, but she did.

The time flashed on the screen. Roughly two and a half hours since she'd been pulled over.

She desperately wanted to call Matthew, but she most needed an attorney. *Please don't let this call go to voice mail*, she prayed.

The number was Diana's mobile phone and she answered.

"This is Alexa. I...seem to have been arrested. I was pulled over and they found a gun that had been planted in my car. Can you come?"

The response was a growl before Diana said, "Are you at the Broadway Ave. station?"

"Yes."

"I'm on my way. I assume you haven't answered questions of any kind."

"All I've done is insist on making a phone call."

"Good. See you in—"

"Can you call Matthew?" Alexa asked. "Tell him what happened?"

"Yeah." Diana sounded gentle. "He may be a lot closer than I am."

Alexa's eyes burned, but let them see her cry again? No.

EVEN FROM THE BACK, Matthew recognized Rick Shanahan's swagger. It couldn't be an accident he'd just appeared from an office right by the holding rooms.

"Shanahan," Matthew snapped.

The guy turned. His surprise was so obviously faked, Matthew had to curl his fingers into a fist to keep from grabbing the SOB's shirt collar and twisting until he confessed what part he'd played in this latest stage set.

"Did you bring in Ms. Adams?"

"Yeah, who told you?"

"Her attorney called me. I did some checking. What in the *hell*?"

"Hey, the woman saw me parked by the road and flipped me off. Took offense from that, you know. So I pulled her over. Unfortunately for her, the gun she'd hidden under her passenger seat had slid out enough for me to see it. What else was I supposed to do but bring her in? Let her shoot me?"

Matthew lowered his voice. "If I find out you set this up, you'll be answering to me. Do you understand?"

Shanahan widened his eyes. "Are you threatening me, Lieutenant?"

"Yeah. I am."

Matthew brushed past him. He didn't bother to look over his shoulder. If Shanahan grabbed him and took a swing, it would be a positive pleasure to take him down.

When he let himself into the holding room and saw Alexa's face, the coal of fury he'd been carrying burst into flame. He let some really nasty words rip.

"I cannot believe—"

She tried to smile. "Me, either. I mean, who reruns a show that sucked the first time around?"

He chuckled, although the flicker of humor did nothing to quell the raging blaze in his chest. Tear tracks had dried on her face. One cheek had been scraped almost raw.

Sitting next to her, he asked, "Are you hurt? Besides this?" Making sure his back was to the camera, he gently touched her cheek.

She winced. "I…fell onto my knees. And…then onto my left shoulder. I'm sick to my stomach. Actually, not much of me feels good. Did I mention this was a rerun?"

He bit back an obscenity. "Tell me what happened."

"I was on my way—"

"No, from the beginning. Where were you going?"

So she told him. Brian Danner—or somebody pretending to be him—had called, claiming he wanted to talk to her. Of course, he'd set the meeting place. She'd taken a roundabout route— "I've been trying to be really careful," she said, as if he'd accused her of carelessness.

He nodded reassurance.

She'd had barely a few blocks to go on one of the main drags that ran through Wilden and out to the highway.

"Now I wish I'd thought to circle way around and approach from the other direction." She made a face. "Although I suppose I'd have waited for Danner for a while, and when I gave up and started for home they'd have pulled me over."

"Danner could have been waiting for you inside the restaurant."

Her eyes widened at his noncommittal remark before she saw the tiny jerk of his head toward the camera. He could tell exactly what she was thinking: *he* might have to be careful but she didn't.

"Not a chance. He appeared way too fast and pointed a gun at me." She huffed out a breath. "It was déjà vu. Lights flashing, siren deafening me."

"Shanahan claims you flipped him off and that's why he pulled you over."

Her mouth dropped open. "What? I'm not stupid enough to do something like that even if I had recognized him. Which I didn't until we'd…well, interacted for a while."

"'Interacted'?"

She told him what Shanahan had whispered in her ear, as well as his original gibe when she'd insisted the gun was a plant.

Now, who would want to do something like that to you?

Matthew had to unclench his jaw to say, "Has your car been parked in the driveway at your house at all? Even for a few minutes, while you carried groceries in, say?"

"No!"

Knowing the camera wouldn't show his face, he grinned at her indignation. "We'll check to see whether anyone broke into your garage."

"I don't suppose I can go home."

Wishing he could pull a miracle out of the hat he never wore, Matthew said, "I'm afraid not yet. Your attorney should be here any minute. She'll get things moving." What Matthew knew was that Alexa wouldn't be going home alone, although he decided not to tell her that yet.

Alexa's nod was stout enough, but for a fleeting instant, her expression betrayed that vulnerability she was so determined to hide. "I've never been arrested before."

A little grimly, he said, "This will make one hell of an article in the *Tribune*."

Her chin came up. "Yes, it will."

There was the Alexa he knew and— Loved? Even the thought stole his breath. This was way too soon. It had to be.

He wished he believed himself.

Chapter Thirteen

The gun, it developed, was remarkably lacking in any fingerprints at all.

As Diana suggested sharply, "Consistent with it having been planted in my client's car, as seems obvious happened."

Better yet, Matthew had taken another detective—Joe Agostini—along with him to inspect the side door into Alexa's garage. The dead bolt wasn't closed—in fact, the door was unlocked entirely—but he saw and photographed marks on the hinges. The door had been removed from the frame, it appeared, presumably because that would have made less noise than bashing it in. However, the perpetrator had had trouble putting it back into place.

The indisputable evidence that someone had, in fact, broken into Ms. Adams's garage, along with the lack of fingerprints on the weapon itself, and the previous incidents involving her, had convinced Judge Sutton to nullify any charges. She'd eyed Shanahan and Danner, appearing as the arresting officers, over the top of her readers long enough to unnerve anyone, then nodded curtly.

"Dismissed."

Alexa walked out of the conference room with her attorney, Matthew following.

Behind him, a voice said, "Lieutenant."

He turned, eyebrows raised.

Brian Danner had separated himself from his co-conspirator. "What's she got that would make you back her when she's out to get any cop she can catch who might've made a mistake? Who hasn't made their share?"

"There is nothing between Ms. Adams and me that affects my stance on this campaign to terrorize her." Matthew looked the other man in the eye. He hoped—no, he believed—he was telling the truth. "I'm doing my job. Yes, everyone makes mistakes, including people in law enforcement, but that's not the same thing as willfully breaking the law we were hired—and are morally obligated—to enforce.

"Ms. Adams is focused on officers who have used the cover provided by a badge, a uniform and a gun to steal drugs from the evidence locker, to use unacceptable levels of force because they enjoy it or because they're biased against their victims, or to blackmail women into relationships they can't say no to. Anyone involved in setting her up repeatedly needs to be fired. Do you hear me?"

Danner's lip curled. "The average citizen doesn't get what this job is like. *You* should know better." He walked away.

Matthew let him go.

FEELING AS IF she had to try to declare independence, Alexa said, "Thanks for the offer, but Diana can drive me to my car."

Looking as immovable as a huge block of granite, Matthew shook his head. "We need to talk."

Diana glanced at her phone. "I do have an appointment at three."

Alexa's shoulders sagged. "Fine." She hugged her attorney. "Thanks for running to my rescue."

Diana grinned at her. "Does he get a hug, too?"

Matthew wore a matching grin. "Yeah, do I?"

Alexa rolled her eyes, feeling very teenaged but justified. "Can we go?"

They parted in front of the police station, Diana's heels clicking on the pavement as she hurried away.

"You know you can't have your car back yet, anyway," Matthew said.

Alexa turned. "What?"

"Crime scene people are going over it." He lifted a hand to prevent her from speaking up. "At this point, that's to your advantage. Being that it was likely a cop who planted that gun, there probably won't be any fingerprints. But someone could have been careless opening the car door. The rubber floor mat could hold a print."

"*Likely* a cop?"

"Jim Berkey wasn't a cop." The set of his jaw was hard, the determination dark in his eyes. "Any of the cops you're investigating could have hired or coerced somebody into doing a little dirty work."

She had to nod. Of course, he was right, although

she had a suspicion either Danner or Shanahan would have enjoyed placing that gun in her car, positioning it just so. If only she'd *really* had to slam on her brakes when that kid on the bike had ridden out in front of her. The gun would have come flying from under the seat.

Walking stiffly beside him to his pickup—did that mean he was taking the rest of the day off?—Alexa glanced down at the torn knee of her chinos, barely exposing the gauze covering her scrapes, and the other dirty, gritty knee. Gauze wrapped her hands, too. The medic had cleaned her cheek and dabbed on a disinfectant that stung, but not seen the need to cover the scrape. She hadn't been near a mirror, but she still had a good idea how awful she looked.

"When do you think I'll get my car back?" she asked as she fastened her seat belt.

"A day or two." He started the engine but didn't shift into Reverse. Instead, he turned his head to meet her eyes. "I don't want you driving."

"But… I have to keep doing my job or they win."

"Would the newspaper provide a car and driver for you?"

"I—" She thought about that. "Maybe." Actually, there was a good chance that, after hearing about today's events, they'd suggest it even without her asking. Or they could reimburse Uber or Lyft charges… except then she'd be accepting rides from strangers, and right now she didn't dare do that.

"I'm going to stay with you," Matthew said, no give

at all in his voice. "In fact, let's go by my place now so I can pack a bag."

She blinked a couple of times as she tried to wrap her mind around the fact that this man was planning to move in with her and clearly had no intention of accepting anything resembling a "no." And she'd only met him…a week ago?

Did she want to say no? A little unnerved, she realized how much she wanted to take him home with her. If he was within earshot, she might be able to sleep without constantly jerking awake at any noise. He wouldn't be able to play bodyguard during the day, of course, but the sight of his pickup parked in her driveway during the night might be enough to serve as a 24/7 deterrent. She could hope.

The worrisome part was that she liked the idea of him spending the night for other reasons. Shutting her bedroom door in his face wouldn't be easy.

She found herself sneaking looks sidelong as he drove. He seemed pensive, although she had no doubt he was alert. Her gaze dropped to his strong hands, wrists and forearms. Those powerful hands wrapped the steering wheel in a relaxed grip. She flashed back again to the man who'd already been stripping off his leather jacket as he'd walked toward her in that awful alley, his first thought to shield her. Had he known how comforting that coat was, too, with the warm sheepskin lining that she realized in retrospect smelled faintly of him?

Once he pulled into a driveway leading to a shabby detached garage beside a stately, two-story home decorated with obviously restored gingerbread and a broad front porch, Alexa gave way to temptation in another way and accompanied him into the house for what he described as the basic tour.

The staircase rose from a central hall. The living room lay to one side, irresistible with gleaming wood floors and moldings, creamy walls and a fireplace mantel carved from solid oak. A lion's head was frozen midroar at each end of the mantel.

She had to be gaping. "Did you do all this work by yourself?" she asked.

"A lot of it." He gazed around, as if appraising the result anew. Although a slight curl at the corner of his mouth suggested that he liked her reaction. "I've recruited a few minions."

Smiling, she said, "Your brother."

Matthew grinned. "Yeah, there's a reason he can hardly wait to get away to college."

"Friends, too, I suppose."

His expression closed so quickly, she knew she'd taken a misstep.

"Not…" She couldn't finish.

"Art? Yeah. We're good friends. I'm hoping…"

"Has there been any more news?"

"I'd dropped by the hospital when your attorney called. Art hasn't regained consciousness yet, but he's getting restless. I wish I were as convinced as his wife is—" He grimaced, turned abruptly and walked back into the hall.

Alexa followed, seeing a dining room with a built-in buffet that was still waiting for the kind of intensive stripping and refinishing that had awed her in the living room, then a half-complete kitchen.

"I mostly had to take this room down to the studs," Matthew said, having regained his composure. "Unfortunately, it had been remodeled a couple of times before. The last was in the seventies. Ugliest vinyl flooring you've ever seen, and the countertop was pretty bad, too. Whatever had been here originally was long gone."

"There probably *wasn't* much here," she pointed out. "The pantry and a wood-burning stove might have been it."

"Yeah, the pantry is good."

He left her to wander around to her heart's content while he went upstairs to throw a few things into a bag, as he put it. She did admire and envy a sizable pantry, peek at a half-bath under the stairs that had been beautifully restored, and a home office, also done. It seemed he'd started with the downstairs. His complaints about plumbing made her wonder if he hadn't also tackled an upstairs bathroom, but it was just as well he hadn't invited her up with him.

Except, of course, that he was coming home with her, instead.

When he came downstairs, his face was stern. All cop, he said, "The gun found in your car is being sent to the state lab. There was talk about test shooting it here, but I shut that down. I want it examined by outsiders."

He hated saying that, and Alexa understood why. He was admitting to her that he couldn't entirely trust anyone in his own department. Without that trust, how could he do his job?

"Was there any objection to using the state lab?" she asked.

He locked his front door and they started toward his truck. "Some pushback from above." There was deep reserve in his voice. "No reason to think the gun had been used in any major crime, I was told. I said there was plenty of reason."

Alexa climbed into the truck, dropped her handbag and stared at him. "You think that was the gun used…" She couldn't quite bring herself to finish.

Matthew did it for her. "To shoot Art. Yes, I do. They had to be setting you up for something bigger than a concealed weapons charge. If we're right that all of this is tied together, putting you in possession of a gun used to kill a cop makes for a harder hit. Right now, that's my best guess."

Feeling sick, Alexa stared straight ahead through the windshield while Matthew drove. If what he feared was true, that meant one of those men had set out to cold-bloodedly shoot a fellow officer. How else had he acquired that particular handgun?

Which one of the four who'd mocked and mistreated her was the killer? They'd obviously joined together to set her up.

"If that's true," she said slowly, "were they all in on trying to go after Detective Dwyer?"

His sideways glance let Alexa see eyes that looked more like molten metal, burning hot, than hardened steel.

"Hard to say." His hands tightened on the steering wheel until it creaked and his knuckles showed white. "But they seem to have all been in on the plan to eliminate *you*."

A little sick turned into a lot sick. If in fact that gun had been used by a killer, she wasn't off the hook yet. How could investigators *not* look at her?

Given that Lieutenant Matthew Reinert headed major crime investigations for the Wilden City Police Department, she had to ask herself how solid his support for her really was—and how she could have the faith in him that she did.

MATTHEW LAY ON his back in the guest bedroom, too occupied brooding to so much as think about sleeping.

Learning that Mike Swartz had been one of the four officers in on Alexa's arrest had disturbed Matthew. That meant three of the four were on both Alexa's and Art's list of problem officers who'd had relations with prostitutes. The name of the fourth guy, Josh Barry, hadn't pinged any alarms for Alexa. Matthew hadn't seen it in Art's notes, either. It was conceivable Barry had simply been patrolling in the area and responded to a request for backup. Matthew intended to talk to him first thing in the morning. He'd already checked to be sure the guy was working. If Barry hadn't wondered at all about the way Alexa was treated, the corruption in the department went deeper than even Matthew had begun to suspect.

He'd be sitting down with the other three, as well,

even if they weren't under his direct command. If he had to stalk them in the parking lot, he'd do that.

He had a hard time believing the three—leaving Josh Barry aside for the moment—had conspired to murder a fellow cop. More likely, they'd come together to take Alexa down a notch because they were like-minded SOBs. Or they knew they were all on her radar and couldn't afford for her to trumpet their sins to the entire city.

They wouldn't have even needed to learn specifics about her records requests; she'd presumably called each officer with a request to sit down with her and discuss the problematic conduct that had been alleged to her. That, of course, had made it easy to set her up the way they had today.

A powerful sense of urgency had been driving Matthew since he'd gotten the call today from Alexa's attorney. Setting that kind of trap was a careless move. Reckless, even, and not so smart. Less so if Matthew was wrong about the gun and it hadn't fired the bullet that intended to kill Art, of course. Otherwise, those three men had turned the spotlight on themselves.

What he couldn't dismiss was the possibility that someone else entirely had given them a nudge, expressing the wish into a willing ear that there was a way to keep up the pressure on that nosy journalist. *How dare she go after us, when she has no clue what it takes to do our jobs?*

Yeah, it could have happened that way. With a groan, Matthew sat up, thinking he'd turn on the light and make some notes, but stopping himself before he reached for the switch on the lamp.

He had to get some sleep. His thoughts had begun to spin in circles, which wasn't helpful. Unfortunately, his acute state of wakefulness had as much to do with the real, live Alexa as it did with the investigation that involved her.

To start with, he didn't like leaving her alone tomorrow, or any day. So far, her enemy had tried to avoid murder. Shooting a cop had been brazen; if Alexa was killed right afterward, along with the tipster responsible for several incidents, even Chief Paulson would be forced to connect the dots.

At least, Matthew would like to think so.

Knowing she was too smart to take unnecessary risks should be more reassuring than it was. And, yes, he understood why she refused to give up her quest, but she'd spoken to the *Tribune* publisher late this afternoon, and he had readily agreed to provide a car and driver for business and personal errands.

Matthew had heard him say, "If you need groceries, have a doctor appointment, anything, don't try to get yourself there. I'll insist on a single driver, so you won't have any doubts when he shows up."

Matthew intended to protect her during any personal errands, but he'd been glad to hear her employers weren't stinting with their backup.

It really wasn't her arrangements for tomorrow keeping him awake, though. Their evening together had been unexpectedly comfortable, spiced with the physical attraction he could never entirely shut down when he was with her. In occasional furtive glances, he'd read wariness, but that was understandable given how he had bulled his way into staying nights at her house.

Now she lay in bed one wall away from the guest bedroom where he was supposed to be sleeping. It didn't help that he knew exactly how enticing she looked beneath her practical everyday garb.

He groaned and slapped the pillow down on his face. He had a ways to go before there was any hope of being invited into her bed.

He growled under the pillow and forced himself also to remember the bruises and swelling, the torn flesh on her wrists and the shock and fear on her face.

He concentrated instead on the relief and welcome that had lit her face at the sight of him when he'd walked into the holding cell.

Chapter Fourteen

Late morning, Diana called to announce that she'd
quit with the foot-dragging and officially notified
everyone concerned that Monday morning she was
filing a lawsuit that lumped together the ambush and
assault as well as the two traffic stops and the planted
gun. She'd be requesting damages, too.

"Unless the department mounts a serious attempt to
identify any individual officers behind this campaign
of terror," she declared, "it will become apparent that,
in fact, WPD as a whole is responsible for it. And,
given their failure to promptly respond when it comes
to your records requests, an unbiased observer—say,
a juror—won't be able to help concluding that this has
all come about because they're afraid to have anyone
shine a light on the conduct of many of their officers.
Which includes several, at the very least, who should
never have been hired in the first place."

Phone to her ear, Alexa exclaimed, "How beautifully put. Thank you."

"You're welcome." A smile could be heard in the
attorney's voice.

"How much money are we asking for in damages?"

The answer was so staggering, her mouth dropped open. "Well," she finally croaked.

"Naturally, we're sticking to our initial goal of oiling the gates leading to the records that are being withheld. But this has gone way beyond that now. I'm trying to scare the you-know-what out of Reggie Paulson, not to mention the mayor and city council members who either think racist, brutal and corrupt policing is the way to go, or else are sticking their collective heads in the sand."

Alexa blinked. "I'm so glad I picked *you* out during my search."

Her attorney laughed. "If we actually win that full settlement..."

"I'll throw the pro bono thing out the window. Promise."

After having such a good night's sleep, courtesy of the comfort of Matthew's presence only a wall away, and now this conversation, Alexa found herself in an astonishingly good mood.

JOSH BARRY SAT stiffly in front of Matthew's desk, but he hadn't seemed reluctant when Matthew caught him on the way in the door and asked for a few minutes before he set out on his usual patrol shift.

"The stop yesterday?" Barry sounded a little puzzled but also uneasy.

"Yes."

"I didn't know the driver was Alexa Adams until I got back to the station after my shift was over. I mean, I wasn't the arresting officer, so once Officer Shanahan loaded her to bring her back here, I took up my patrol where I'd left off."

Matthew nodded. "Did anything that happened once you arrived at the scene appear out of the norm?"

A short, solid guy in his late twenties, Barry squirmed. "Ah…well, I almost pulled my sidearm because two of the other three already had, but then I saw a petite woman, alone, who appeared to already have been subdued. In fact, I don't know why they needed me, but Shanahan asked for my continued backup." He fell silent but a nerve in his cheek twitched.

Matthew gave him some time.

"Unless she really fought before I arrived, I thought they were rough with her," he blurted out. "Once she was out of the car, there was no need to throw her down or cuff her ankles."

"Now that you know who she is, do you have any thoughts on why the stop occurred, and why they were so hard on her?"

Barry surged almost to his feet before sinking back down. "Everyone knows she's investigating people in our department. She wants to dump on our reputation."

Matthew raised his eyebrows. "*Our*?"

Holding a hint of desperation, brown eyes met his. "That's…what they're all saying."

"All? Or only the officers guilty of misconduct the public wouldn't condone? Misconduct that's been swept under the rug?" He let his voice harden. "I'd argue those are the officer who actually *are* blackening our reputation, shaming the men and women who do this job honorably."

Barry grimaced. "Maybe most of us keep our heads down more than we should, but I agree with you, and I think the majority of the guys do, too. I hear and see things…"

"Brian Danner was your FTO." Field training officers had an outsize influence on rookies.

"Yeah, uh, I think things went on he didn't let me see. I mean mostly he was okay, you know?"

They both knew what he was saying. Reporting your FTO for conduct unbefitting a law enforcement officer wasn't the way to find acceptance and guidance when joining a police force.

"Are you usually on the same shift as Danner? Or either of the others, for that matter."

He nodded. "Since I came off nights six weeks ago. But—" another hesitation "—Shanahan and Danner were both on my turf. Unless they were on break, meeting someone for lunch or coffee. Shanahan was supposed to be downtown, and Danner… I'm not sure." His expression eased. "It was lunchtime, though, so probably he and the others *were* meeting up, and that's why they were all so close by when he put out the call."

Yep. They'd arranged to meet up, all right, but not at a coffee shop or café. Matthew saw Josh Barry's face tighten again as he, too, saw the unwelcome possibility.

"What do you want, Lieutenant?" he demanded suddenly.

"Honesty. I needed to know if you were part of what they were up to—and I need you to keep your mouth shut about what I'm suspecting."

"I heard the call for backup. That's all."

"That's what I needed to know," Matthew said, rising to his feet. "Thank you for your honesty."

Barry nodded and stood, too. He appeared to have aged since he'd walked into the office. Getting your eyes opened to the evil hiding in plain sight had a way of doing that to you, Matthew thought.

THE CRIME SCENE report concluded that the gunman who'd shot Art Dwyer had stood by the detached garage off the alley. Making a shot from that distance— one that missed by only a hair—suggested unusual capability. Reality was, too many cops didn't keep their skills up. Matthew had an interesting conversation with the police range master.

Of the original list of five WPD officers who interested both Alexa and Art—and leaving aside, for the moment, John Blykowski, the sheriff's deputy, Rick Shanahan and Don Rommel were the most diligent at keeping their skills sharp at the shooting range. Brian Danner trailed them, but was, in the words of the range master, "Okay."

"I wouldn't mind having him back me up." Ed Lee was a retired cop. "But he's not on the level of Shanahan and Rommel. They have some kind of competition going. They can both empty the magazine and gut the bull's-eye without a single wandering shot. Steady hands." He shook his head. "I worry that they're too cocky."

The description didn't surprise Matthew. The attitude was one of the things he didn't like about several of those officers. Sure, confidence was a requisite for this job, but you also had to believe in the rule of law, understand that you were employed by the citizens of your city. A decent man never let himself forget that the lowest dirtbag you arrested was a human being.

Ed Lee went on to say that Ken Kasperson came in often enough to maintain his middling skill and certification. Mike Swartz showed rarely, usually in company with a friend.

That could mean he went to another range, or, if he lived out of town, even had one set up on his own property.

Instinct had Matthew wanting to corner Shanahan and the others without warning, and without sending any signals up the command structure. That would mean cutting out Sergeant Estevez, who supervised patrol officers on the day shift. Matthew knew how he'd feel if the tables were turned. Sergeant Enrico Estevez's solid reputation helped with his decision.

Taking the risk, Matthew went to Estevez's office midmorning. He already knew the patrol sergeant's workweek was Tuesday through Saturday, so he should be in.

Enrico Estevez had a thin build, a face sculpted like a Mayan frieze, and a booming voice that never required any help from a bullhorn. That voice could make the biggest, toughest guy freeze.

He frowned when he saw who his visitor was. Matthew explained bluntly that he'd like to interview Swartz, Shanahan and Danner.

The sergeant's eyes narrowed. "This have to do with that traffic stop yesterday?" he finally said.

"In part. Their names keep popping up in an investigation of mine."

Eyebrows climbed.

"Art Dwyer's shooting," Matthew said reluctantly. "Plus the…attempts to scare off Ms. Adams, the journalist." He'd never gotten even a whiff of anything off in Estevez's past, but their paths hadn't crossed much to date.

The sergeant leaned forward. "You're suggesting—?"

"I'm having to consider the possibility that Art was targeted by a fellow cop. Yes." Matthew told him why.

The lines on Estevez's forehead deepened, if anything, as he visibly checked for flaws in the logic of Matthew's argument. His next words suggested he hadn't found any.

Estevez gave a brusque nod. "Yeah, I'm okay with you talking to those guys. I hope like hell you're wrong, but I can't argue with your reasoning. I was already unhappy about yesterday's stop. Don't know if you've heard that Ms. Adams's attorney is filing a lawsuit that would damn near bankrupt this county. Yesterday was apparently the kicker after the load of garbage she's already been handed."

"Ms. Adams is investigating three of the four officers involved yesterday."

"Is she."

The flat, unsurprised response told Matthew that Sergeant Estevez knew about conduct that justified a journalist's investigation. Matthew guessed that the conduct had either occurred before Estevez had been transferred to command of the men in question, or that he'd been overruled when he tried to rein in Danner, Shanahan and Swartz.

Matthew had no trouble envisioning Chief Paulson deciding that boys would be boys and shouldn't be held accountable.

"Good," he said, pushing himself to his feet.

"They're all coming in early from their shifts. I'd intended to sit them down. You can have them instead." Estevez gave a tight smile. "I'll separate them to be sure they don't have a chance to coordinate their version of events." The smile turned into a grimace. "At least, any more than they already have."

Matthew felt good about the sergeant as he took the stairs up a level to the major crimes unit. He wasn't thrilled to have to wait until nearly the end of the day for those interviews, but it wasn't as if he didn't have plenty to do today to keep him occupied—there were alibis to pursue, not to mention scheduling a talk with Officer Alan Sharpe's widow.

ALEXA LIKED HER assigned driver right away.

"Don't worry," he said when he got out to meet her

in her driveway. He held open the back door of the large SUV for her. "I can't move fast on my feet, but I'm a hell of a driver."

She evaluated him briefly, liking what she saw. Tall and lanky, he looked to be in his forties and wore a wedding ring.

"Can I sit in front with you?" she asked.

He grinned. "Sure thing." He held out a hand. "Vince Rowan."

"Alexa Adams." They shook.

"I already knew that."

She laughed, buckled her seat belt and said, "Can you make sure we're not followed?"

His eyes sharpened. "Absolutely."

"Give me a minute, then."

Olivia Sharpe answered the phone promptly. She sounded surprised at Alexa's request but agreed that she was free now. "Come right over."

Alexa had intended to go to her home-away-from-home at the library, where she had privacy, quiet, and the comforting awareness that she wasn't quite alone, saving the conversation with the killed officer's widow until a phone call this evening. But now that she had a second pair of watchful eyes, she thought it might be safe to visit instead of rely on a phone call. She'd been afraid that, if her nemesis knew she'd tied Sharpe's death to the attack on Art Dwyer, he'd redouble his effort to shut her up.

Not that Danner and Shanahan and company

could afford to have her house watched 24/7…but she couldn't poke her nose outside without wondering.

She gave the address to her new driver, watched as he entered it in the GPS, then sat back for the ride across town.

The house wasn't hard to find. A rambler, it reminded her of her own, except the homeowner had not just a green thumb, but time for serious gardening. Roses rioted over porch railings. Fragrant masses of lavender and a lot of other perennials Alexa didn't recognize filled deep flower beds between rose stems.

"I doubt I'll be here long," Alexa said as she opened her door.

"Wait," Vince told her. "Why don't you let me take a look around before you get out?"

Bemused, she hovered inside her open door until he got out, strolled as far as the street and stuck his head around the corner of the garage, so he knew what was between houses, before he finally came around to escort her to the walkway leading to the front door.

Alexa eyed him. "So, you're not just a driver, you're a bodyguard?"

Humor gone, he said, "I'm unarmed, but you're not the first client I've chauffeured who fears being followed."

Sure enough, at the deep-throated sound of an approaching vehicle, he stepped in front of her.

They both watched a black pickup pull into the driveway right behind the hired SUV. With a sense of inevitability, Alexa saw Lieutenant Matthew Reinert exit his vehicle, cast a quick glance at her and walk toward them with a now-hard gaze fixed on her escort.

"WE SHARED THE desktop computer," Olivia said nervously, her eyes flicking between Alexa and Matthew. "He had a work laptop, of course, but they took that. And the phone."

Alexa had trouble believing that a man as alarmed as Sharpe had been, ordered by his supervisors to forget what he'd seen, wouldn't have left notes somewhere. After all, this was a guy desperate enough to consider confiding in someone outside his department. No, not just someone specifically, a journalist, who would certainly not have kept quiet about whatever he'd told her.

If he kept notes…well, in times past, she thought ruefully, he'd have hidden them beneath the false bottom of a drawer, or the like. Now, however, they almost had to be digital.

If he'd said anything incendiary to friends, wouldn't you think one of them would have come forward after he was murdered?

And would he have told a friend something he *hadn't* told his wife?

Or *had* he talked to Olivia?

If the friend was also a cop, though, could he have been involved in whatever wrongdoings Sharpe had observed, or, at least, been stubbornly blind to them?

Blind enough not to wonder given Sharpe was murdered so soon after, though?

Alexa had considered the possibility that Olivia

did know why her husband had been killed and kept quiet because of threats. Although, you'd think she'd have moved away if that were the case.

After meeting the woman, Alexa just couldn't see it.

"Did he spend much time on the computer here at home?" Matthew asked. He'd been a rather quiet presence thus far, although a man with his size and commanding air was hard to ignore. Now, it went without saying that he'd seen right away where Alexa was going with her questions.

"Well...yes," the pretty blonde said. "But when he was working, it was always with the laptop." She seemed to have trouble pulling her gaze from the enormous, framed portrait of her husband hanging over the fireplace, or maybe it was from the half dozen other photos displayed on the mantel.

"Was he into computer games? Or did he mostly email?" Alexa asked.

"Not games. But emails, sure. I mean, sometimes, but we both grew up locally and saw our friends and family often. That's why I decided to stay here in town after. It's hard, because everywhere I look, there's a memory of us together, but—" She broke off.

"This is where your support network is," Alexa said softly.

Olivia's smile seemed grateful. "Yes."

"So?" Matthew was undoubtedly trying for patience but beginning to fall short.

"So...? Oh! The computer. He was writing a book," she explained. "He loved Joseph Wambaugh. That kind of mystery."

Hiding her tension and excitement, Alexa said, "How far along was he?"

"Halfway, maybe? He kept getting ideas and going back, so he wasn't progressing very fast."

Matthew's eyes met Alexa's. It was a little alarming that she could read his message. *She'll respond better to you than me.* He must have sensed that from the beginning.

"Have you read the manuscript?" she asked as gently as she could.

"Some of it when he first started writing," Olivia said. "But that's not the kind of stuff I read, so I couldn't do much but be encouraging."

"Since he died?"

Her lips compressed. "Even thinking about it makes me sad."

"Would you permit us to do so?" Seeing instant wariness on Olivia's face, Alexa reminded her, "You're aware that he called me before his death because he'd seen something he'd thought was wrong and nobody within the department would pay attention to him. It's conceivable that while he had his manuscript open, he played with ideas about what to do about the problem that was worrying him. Made pro and con lists. Things like that."

Increasingly distressed, Sharpe's wife cried, "But he never dreamed anyone would kill him over what he saw!"

Matthew spoke up. "All I can tell you is that we're revisiting the investigation into his death because there are definite parallels with how and why Art

Dwyer was shot. I need to pursue any possibility. I'd be grateful if you can help. Bad enough that someone thinks he got away with killing an officer of the law. But now...if he's tried to do it again?"

Let's not forget Tansy Gould and the other young women, Alexa thought. Although she didn't believe for a minute that Matthew had forgotten them. His goal was maximum emotional punch on this widow, who now stared at him in shock.

Chapter Fifteen

"I don't—didn't—really know Art," Olivia said hesitantly, "but when my son was born, Art's wife called out of the blue. She gave us a stroller, crib bedding and a ton of clothes because she said they'd decided not to try for a third baby. It was such a blessing. I'd had to quit my job." Blue eyes wet, she looked at Matthew. "I should call her. Do you have her number?"

"I do." He swallowed. "I think Michelle would be really grateful to hear from you. She's hanging on to hope, but it's hard."

Olivia's hands curled into fists. "I'll do anything I can to help you catch the monster who killed Alan. I can email you the manuscript. Would that do?"

"Yes. Thank you."

Alexa didn't say anything, but she was thinking it: he'd darned well better share a copy with her. What she did say was, "While you're at it, you might take another look at any other documents created in the month or so before his death, read emails he sent out, hunt for unexpected activity. You may have done that at the time, but with some distance, you have a fresh eye now."

Olivia nodded firmly. "I will."

Thank God, she hadn't replaced the computer yet, Alexa couldn't help thinking.

"Did the detectives who spoke to you at the time ask to look at your home computer?" Matthew asked.

Olivia frowned a little. "No. No, they seemed to think someone he'd arrested had killed him in revenge."

"That's still possible," Matthew conceded, "but I'm no longer convinced."

Teary-eyed again, she walked them to the door and, accepting Matthew's card, promised to email the manuscript immediately. Matthew entered Michelle Dwyer's number in Olivia's phone before thanking her again for her time and cooperation.

Vince waited outside, leaning against the SUV. Apparently, her driver had passed Matthew's test once they'd exchanged a few words.

"How'd it go?" he asked, straightening.

"Fingers crossed," Alexa said. "I think I'll head to the library next."

Matthew frowned. "I don't like you being isolated in back the way you were the day I stopped by."

She rolled her eyes. "I'm not isolated. People wander in and out through the stacks. The back door is kept locked, and Vince will be waiting out front."

Matthew frowned but gave a short nod. "Okay. Want me to bring something home for dinner?"

Home? Really? Heat tinged her cheeks at Vince's interested expression.

"I'll find something. But I'd better have a copy of

that manuscript in my inbox by the time I open my email account."

He had the nerve to hesitate. "This is part of a homicide investigation, only indirectly linked to your research into problem officers."

Alexa took a step forward to get right in his face. "I got here first. In fact—" she scowled "—how'd you know I was going to see Olivia?"

Matthew's mouth quirked. "Maybe great minds think alike."

She didn't so much as blink.

"I called to make an appointment to see her today. She told me you were coming. I figured it would be easier for her to get it all out once."

He could be thoughtful, but call her cynical. He just hadn't wanted her learning something he hadn't.

Her stare was evidently getting to him because he snapped, "Fine!" *He* stepped forward until only inches separated them and she had to tip her head back to keep glowering at him. "But you keep anything you see to yourself, is that clear? Arresting this piece of scum for murder is the priority, not your front-page headline."

Alexa would have liked to see heat blisters popping out on Matthew's lean cheeks, but a woman couldn't get everything she wanted. Without another word to him, she swung around and stalked to the passenger side of the SUV.

Vince was behind the wheel before she managed to close her door. Reading her mood, he gave her a sidelong glance. "We'll have to wait for the lieutenant to back out."

She snorted.

"Don't know that I've ever heard of a reporter and a homicide detective working a case together."

"We're not. Exactly."

"Kind of sounded like you are."

"He—and I—think the person out to get me also murdered one cop and tried to kill another."

"Ah." Vince closed his hands around the wheel and gazed out the windshield for a minute, even though Matthew had already backed into the street. "Art Dwyer and Alan Sharpe."

"Yes." She turned her head to look at him. "You knew?"

"I follow the news," Vince said simply. His eyes met hers. "Maybe I shouldn't say this, but it seems to me he has a point."

She huffed out a breath. "About our priority? Of course he does. What irritates me is that he'd think for a minute I'd rather get a spectacular headline than see that…that *monster* behind bars."

Vince looked over his shoulder and accelerated out of the driveway. "I imagine cops get cautious for a reason."

Unwilling to trust that people will act from their better natures?

Alexa bumped her head a couple of times on the seat back. "I get that."

That was only one of many reasons why Matthew shouldn't be making himself *at home* with her.

And why she shouldn't get used to having him there.

MATTHEW WAS STILL seething when he let himself in Alexa's front door with the key she'd given him that morning in case their schedules didn't coordinate. The key he'd added to his chain with great satisfaction.

"It's me," he called and followed the sound of a pan banging onto a stove into the kitchen.

He caught a flash of emotion in her eyes when she glanced at him, but couldn't decipher it. He did drink in the sight of her slim, utterly feminine body and fine-boned, stubborn face.

She didn't greet him with any great enthusiasm but asked, "Black bean quesadillas okay?"

"Yeah." Despite his dark mood, he kissed her on the cheek, enjoying the soft give, before backing away. "Last thing today, I talked to those sons of bitches who arrested you. Got nowhere, and I'd swear they were all smirking on their way out of my office."

Just as Art had described Jim Ward, O'Brien and their buddies, come to think of it. He might have narrowed his list too soon—except those two had been fired. He'd like to think they were frantically job hunting with no success.

Still, someone who hadn't risen to his attention could have incited Shanahan and company, he had to remind himself.

Alexa made a scoffing noise. "Why aren't I shocked?"

He scraped a hand over his jaw. "The better question is why am I?"

She summoned a crooked smile for him. "Because you're an optimist?"

Matthew's anger relented, leaving him able to laugh. "That's me." He nodded toward the cutting board she'd set out on the counter. "Can I do anything?"

"No, this is really simple. My go-to dinner when I don't have a lot of time."

He sipped a beer and they talked as she dumped two cans of beans along with salsa and corn into a saucepan and set it to simmering. A minute later, she added diced bell peppers and some spices. It seemed neither of them was eager to talk about the frustration engendered by reading what messages had been left to them from beyond the grave by Officer Alan Sharpe, because neither raised the subject. Alexa told him she hadn't stayed long at the library because she'd felt guilty leaving the driver sitting in the parking lot.

She shrugged. "I mean there's no reason to think I'm not safe here."

Matthew wished he believed that. The brutality of the first attack made it clear that Alexa having been set up repeatedly wasn't only the actions of some dirty cops afraid they'd lose their jobs if she pursued her investigation and their names appeared in the *Tribune*. Those cops had gone way beyond nasty tricks. They must know how quickly any of those incidents could have turned tragic and either hadn't cared or had hoped for her death.

He came right out with it. "I got results on the ballistics today. They put a rush on it because we suspected the gun had been used in the attempted murder of a cop and the shooting of another one."

She went very still. The green in her hazel eyes had darkened. "It was used to shoot Art?"

Matthew bent his head. "Art and Alan Sharpe as well as Jim Berkey." He reminded her that Berkey had been responsible for the tip leading to the raid on her house. "Tansy Gould and the others, we don't know."

They hadn't recovered bullets from the bodies or the garbage dumpsters.

The results from the state lab tied in a neat knot the parallels between her investigation and Art's, and the not-so-coincidental fact that Jim Berkey had been murdered, his body disposed of in the same way several prostitutes had met their ends.

Alexa nodded and seemed to withdraw. He couldn't blame her.

"Michelle thinks Art is going to open his eyes any minute," he reported, voice rough from the hope he tried to keep in check. "Doctor is optimistic. Nobody is talking about whether he could have suffered brain damage."

Alexa only nodded again, looking even more somber. She served the melted cheese and black bean quesadillas at the table, along with asparagus and a tub of sour cream.

He'd already taken a bite when she picked up then set down her fork and looked at him, all her frustration in her expression.

"Did you read it?"

"Yeah."

"Why didn't he name names?" she exclaimed. Or maybe she was begging for an explanation.

Matthew had immediately known why Sharpe hadn't identified fellow officers even as he'd read the shocked paragraph describing the three of them ushering hookers away from a hotel just before an operation was sprung. Seeing some groping, and fright more than gratitude on the faces of the women. And then the one cop who had been assigned to participate in the sting had melted back into his place, confident nobody had seen.

Until Alan Sharpe had started telling his tale and getting shut down. Even so, the three officers had had to ask themselves…what if someone eventually *did* listen?

Sharpe was dead less than a week later.

Murder was a damned extreme reaction in the circumstances. Getting caught being involved with prostitutes would likely not have resulted in more than a slap on the hand, which was apparently the norm these days for WPD. Maybe a reprimand. Unfortunately, one of those three men, at the very least, had to be protecting darker secrets. If anybody had seriously started looking into the guy's history with prostitutes, he might have been connected to the series of murders.

"Sharpe was still struggling with his loyalties," Matthew said. "We stand up for each other. Keep our mouths shut. What he saw wasn't so terrible. Yeah, he disapproved of law enforcement officers getting involved with women who broke the law every day, and especially of the married guys. But he didn't see anyone get hurt."

"Except, he wondered," Alexa said tautly. "The women were being saved from an arrest—"

"Probably not their first."

"And he thought they were every bit as afraid of the men 'helping them' as they would have been of spending a night in jail and adding a charge to their records."

"To his credit, that's why Sharpe decided to speak out. He just never imagined…" Matthew shook his head.

"No." Alexa looked down at her plate for a long moment then started to eat.

She'd cleared her plate before she stormed, "It's maddening! Having our suspicions confirmed, but with the creeps still anonymous. And I can't help thinking those three may be just the tip of the iceberg. There could be half a dozen more officers doing the same thing. I mean I've gotten tips about at least a couple more."

"Art had others on his list, too," Matthew agreed. "But we know that one of the three officers Sharpe saw was our target and the man out to shut you up." *No matter what.*

Alexa had to be thinking the same, but she responded as if this were an intellectual problem, not a personal one. "Because why would he have murdered a fellow officer if *his* name wasn't one of those Sharpe would have shared with his sergeant or whoever he went to?"

"Exactly. And I know for a fact that Sharpe spoke both to his sergeant and to the lieutenant above him, even though jumping above the sergeant's head must have caused some tension. My best guess is that they both told him more might have been going on than he realized, and the men and women he worked with needed to be able to trust him. If they couldn't, maybe he should quit his job."

Alexa's chin came up. She vibrated with sudden aggression. "What if one of your detectives came to you with suspicions about a coworker? Would you say the same thing?"

Stunned, Matthew stared at her. Damn. That was what she still thought about him? He'd been an idiot to be falling for her, to love sharing breakfast and dinner with her even if he hadn't made it into her bed yet—

Her face convulsed. "I'm sorry! I don't know why I even said that! No, I do. I keep trying to—"

When she didn't finish, he prodded, "To what?"

Cheeks glowing hot, she was too gutsy to avoid meeting his gaze. "Protect myself, I guess. Not like I know what you have in mind, I mean about—" she flapped a hand in a gesture meant to encompass the two of them "—but since it wouldn't work anyway..."

"You're afraid," he said slowly.

"No! I'm just..."

"Afraid." He shook his head when she opened her mouth to keep arguing. "*I've* been afraid you'd never be able to trust me. What you just said tells me that maybe you can't."

"No." It was almost a whisper. "I do. What happened wasn't your fault. You haven't let me down. I don't believe you will."

"Every time I have to leave you, I'm afraid he—

they—will get to you." That anguish roughened his voice.

"But our only chance is to keep digging," Alexa protested. "You *have* to go to work."

He wanted to ask her again to go into hiding. To let *him* do the digging. He didn't waste his breath. She wasn't the "running away" kind—and if she were, he wouldn't feel the way about her that he did.

Matthew pushed back his chair and stood. "Alexa."

She rose more slowly, her gaze never leaving his. "This…this still isn't smart."

"I don't care." He held out a hand. "I want you."

He saw her deep breath, her lashes flutter down. And then she walked around the table and laid her small hand in his.

With a gentle pull, he drew her to him. This kiss felt as if it would mean something in a way the others hadn't, but he didn't let himself overthink it. Not when he so desperately wanted her in his arms.

Go easy.

That concept crashed when she threw herself the last short distance to press against him, when she rose on tiptoe and fiercely gripped his shirt as *she* went for his mouth.

Matthew gripped her butt to lift her high enough to wrap her legs around his waist and backed her into the closest wall.

The kiss was openmouthed, sizzling hot, and urgent.

ALEXA HELD OUT as long as she could but finally had to wrench her mouth away to snatch a breath. Nobody had ever kissed her like this, as if her taste was ambrosia. She'd be glad if he never quit, except he was also using his strong hands on her butt to move her up and down, rubbing the most sensitive part of her body against his erection. Increasingly desperate, she tightened her thighs to ride him as if they didn't have several layers of clothing between them.

"*God*." Matthew lifted his head. Dark color ran across his lean cheeks and his eyes were wild. "Alexa. I can't take much more. If this isn't a yes…"

She was too far gone to consult that voice of common sense. She'd wanted this man since the first time she had really let herself see him. But even before, in the alley, his hands had been so gentle when he wrapped his coat around her. The same hands had been strong and competent when he worked on her front door.

She loved those hands.

In fact— No, no, too soon!

She nipped his neck, tasting salt and man. "This is a yes."

Matthew made a strangled sound and hoisted her a little higher. "Hold on tight."

Whether she was being smart or dumb, she needed him. To occupy herself to ensure sure she didn't have time for second thoughts, Alexa tormented him as he carried her out of the kitchen and down the hall. She licked his throat, nibbled his scratchy jaw, and squirmed. Had she ever felt this *needy*?

Panting, he returned the favor by squeezing her butt cheeks and allowing his long fingers to slip lower, to tease and retreat. Given the ridiculously short length of time they'd known each other, she felt as if she'd been waiting for this man forever. If only she was re-acting entirely to his big, solid body and the penetrating gray eyes, to the strength and certainty he exuded, but Alexa knew it was more.

The more that still frightened her.

She didn't notice when they went through the doorway into her bedroom. The first she knew was when those strong hands shifted to her hips so that he could peel her off him and set her on her feet. She had to release her clasp around his neck. He hadn't changed his mind, had he?

He yanked her shirt over her head and tossed it. Question answered. Seconds later, her bra slid down her arms and dropped to the floor. Matthew said a few things that sounded almost prayerful as he enclosed her breasts in his hands then rubbed gently. Even as she arched into his touch, she grabbed the hem of his shirt and tried to lift it.

A momentary struggle ensued; he didn't want to let go of her, but she won. And, oh, his chest, hard belly and powerful shoulders were as beautiful as she'd imagined. The vee of nut-brown hair only emphasized the defined muscles beneath.

They both explored, stroked, squeezed, until he groaned and she let out something like a whimper. He broke, lifting her again to lay her across the bed. He unbuttoned her pants, and with a few wriggles on her part and tugs on his, she was naked. Sprawled, waiting for him.

She'd never seen a man undress that fast. Especially one who had to untie laces, kick off boots and socks and stow a holstered gun, phone and badge on the bedside stand.

Oh, and drop a few packets beside them. Not strictly necessary, but she'd never made love with a man without insisting he use condoms. This time, reaching out to squeeze his impressive erection, she was tempted to tell him to forget sheathing himself. Of course, she wouldn't; she might be bold on the job, but she'd always protected herself personally—both physically and emotionally.

Matthew didn't even ask, though. He put on a condom and came down on top of her. The next thing she knew, they were kissing again as deeply and hungrily as when they'd started. When he took his mouth from hers, she cried, "No!" but he went for her breast instead, licking, suckling, before switching to the other breast. His fingers slid between her folds until she lost it and climbed on top of him.

"Now!"

He laughed up at her, eyes molten, and helped her fit herself to him. And then she rode him, and he rode her, and for the first time in her life, she screamed when her body imploded.

He made a harsh sound and she felt every second of his long, shuddering release.

Chapter Sixteen

"If I thought this would go on long enough, I'd install an alarm system on this house," Matthew said grimly the next morning as he pushed away his empty plate after finishing breakfast.

Alexa looked surprised. Maybe because he'd become a cop instead of her lover a little too abruptly. But what she said was, "You'd install one yourself?"

He hesitated. "Probably not now. I can't afford to get distracted."

"And I'm sure an alarm involves the dreaded electricity," she pointed out.

He grimaced, but playfully, able to relax. "Caught me making an excuse."

Better yet, he'd install a security system on *his* house, and she could move in with him. Not something he could suggest in the near future. He felt more positive than he had in a while this morning, though, thanks to their lovemaking. But also more apprehensive. He hated knowing he wasn't any closer to identifying his man than he'd been two weeks ago.

"What are you doing today?" she asked. Sort of

casually, as a girlfriend or even roommate might ask over the breakfast table, but with a serious undertone he couldn't mistake. "Can you take it off?"

He did take a lot of full weekends off, but under the circumstances? Matthew hesitated. "Unless you need me, I thought I'd put in a few hours and sit with Art to give Michelle and the kids a break. What about you?"

She paused long enough to make him wary. "I have an interview with a cop who I've been browbeating. Not anyone relevant to what's been happening, I'm pretty sure. Vince is driving me, the guy is going to get in the car to talk while Vince sits on a park bench right nearby."

"That should be okay," Matthew conceded grudgingly.

"Then—" She didn't quite meet his eyes. "Late this afternoon, early evening, I'm going to flash some pictures around downtown once the nightlife starts up. I know Sunday night isn't the best, but…"

"You're going to show photos of *cops*?" He'd been wanting to do the same, but knew full well he'd lose his job if he did.

"Sure," Alexa said breezily. "Not ones of them in uniform or anything like that. I've found some on social media sites. You know."

"I'll shadow you."

She shook her head. "You stand out." Now she did survey him, boots to face. "All cop, plus alpha male. You'd scare anyone away who is on the fence about whether to talk or not."

He couldn't afford to be seen canvassing with her,

but he was better at staying out of sight than she guessed. All he said was, "Your driver?"

"He has to stay in the car, but he'll change parking spots to stay close."

"Is he armed?"

"I…doubt it. Would you want him to be?"

Busy as the streets and sidewalks were downtown even on a Sunday when the dinner hour approached and activity in the bars picked up, no. Especially not a guy who was extremely unlikely to put in the number of hours needed to maintain any level of skill with his weapon.

"No. You'll tell me anything you learn?"

"Unless it's unrelated to your investigation." Her eyes narrowed at whatever she saw on his face. "You know I may be investigating cops for a long time to come. I won't let you stop me."

He stood and went around the table, giving her a lopsided grin. As annoyed as she undoubtedly was, when he held out a hand, she laid hers in it and let him pull her to her feet.

"I get that. But you and I both know this is different. We're looking for a killer who thinks *you're* his personal bull's-eye."

Her shoulders sagged. "I haven't forgotten. Why else did I agree to let you stay here?"

He raised his eyebrows. "Is that the only reason?"

She eyed him cautiously. "Well…maybe not."

Not as reassured as he'd like to be, he nodded.

"I just can't let myself be so intimidated I don't fight back," she said in a rush.

And there it was, damn it—one of the reasons she'd drawn him so powerfully from the beginning. Her stubborn refusal to back down, and the will that allowed her to bounce back and defy whoever and whatever had tried to mow her down.

Beneath it all, he'd recognized from the beginning that they had something major in common, too: the need to stand up for right, goodness, justice. And no, he wouldn't put his own motivation in such soppy terms, but it served.

He bent to kiss her. He'd intended to make a point, but he loved the feel of her lips, the hot rush of her breath, her taste, and he got carried away. It wasn't easy to rein himself in, but finally he raised his head and looked down into her dazed eyes.

"Last night was amazing."

Alexa blinked until her gaze was as sharp as usual. Then she smiled. "Yes, it was."

"Good." He kissed her again but didn't linger. "Text me. I want to hear from you regularly today, and especially tonight."

Even if he trailed her, chances were good he'd lose sight of her some of the time.

"Yes, sir!" She saluted.

He grinned and left.

DARRELL WALKER OPENED the back door of Alexa's hired SUV and hopped in. His head turned all the while, something close to panic on his face.

"We should have met somewhere farther out of town."

"What are the odds anyone who knows you will go by? If they did, all they'll see is the back of my head. You could be meeting anyone."

He wasn't that distinctive-looking, she thought. He was handsome in a generic way, stubble darkening his jaw, his head shaved to a stubble, too, like so many other cops around here. At least he didn't have that overmuscled look.

When she reminded him that he'd agreed to her recording the conversation, he said curtly, "Yeah, don't care."

Even though she eased into her questions, Darrell remained tense and defensive. Yeah, he might have been a little rougher with the guy she mentioned than he should have been, but he'd been refusing to get out of the car and Darrell couldn't be sure he didn't have a gun under the seat, say.

"In the body camera footage, it's clear his hands were both on the steering wheel, in compliance with your order."

"But you heard me order him to get out of the car, too, didn't you?"

"I also heard him ask why he'd been pulled over. That seemed like a reasonable question to me."

"He was speeding."

"You didn't use a radar gun."

"I didn't have to. He rocketed by me."

The doctor who'd had to spend the night in the hospital after Darrell Walker threw him to the pavement and kicked him a few times had been positive he hadn't exceeded the speed limit.

"Why didn't you answer his question?"

Darrell glared at her. "I didn't pull him over to chat. He was challenging me."

She kept her expression calm. "You have three other complaints on your record for hurting motorists who either insist they did nothing to justify being pulled over or were pulled over for a minor infraction, such as rolling past a stop sign."

His face set. "My word against theirs."

"As it happens, all four injured complainants are non-white. Can you comment on that?"

"Every one of them refused to follow my clear directions!"

And so it went. Alexa couldn't help wondering why he'd agreed to meet with her, and agreed to allow her to record their conversation.

Eventually, she thanked him for his time and he said, "You know these are all old complaints, right?"

The most recent had been eight months ago—unless there were others that hadn't been included in the file to which she'd been given access.

"I *do* follow orders."

"I'm glad to hear that," she couldn't resist saying.

Hand on the door handle, he said, "Maybe you should write about what *cops* have to put up with every day, turn the spotlight around for once." He leaped out, slammed the door and, with his shoulders hunched and his head down, walked toward his car.

For all that he'd disgusted her, Alexa found herself pondering his suggestion as she moved to the front passenger seat to wait for Vince to get in be-hind the wheel.

It might *be* interesting to listen to the rank and file's stories of abuse they'd accepted with stoicism and unfailing civility. Write an article reminding readers that there were plenty of good cops out there.

ALEXA KNEW HERSELF to be conspicuous although she tried really hard to appear to be ambling along, checking out different bars, even stopping to read the menus a couple of restaurants posted in their front windows. The growing darkness helped in one way, but not in another. Sometimes enough light fell through the windows of a restaurant or tavern to allow the few women who even pretended to look at the pictures to see them. Otherwise, she had to aim for corners, where the streetlights stood.

So far, she was striking a big fat zero, except for the giveaway twitches that told her the women were lying. Vince wasn't very happy now that it was getting dark and he was having trouble tracking her.

For the second time in about two minutes, her phone dinged.

Yep, him again. Time to quit?

Not yet, she responded.

Up ahead, she spotted two girls at the corner, both wearing skirts that barely covered their butts—butts they made the most of when they took a few steps to flaunt themselves at passersby while smiling an in-vitation at single, male drivers.

Alexa glanced back just as the light down the street

changed, causing a lull in traffic. Only during those brief breaks could she get any of the women she approached to so much as hear her beginning spiel.

That, by the way, had changed.

Alexa approached these two with a "Hey. Do you have a second?"

Both swung around to appraise her, and obviously concluded she wasn't any competition. She hid her instinctive horror at seeing how young they were, especially the blond girl. For all the makeup and posturing, she couldn't be more than fifteen or sixteen, and maybe even younger than that.

"My name's Alexa," she told them. "I'm looking for a guy who killed my sister." She'd given up on being honest about being a reporter for the *Spokane Valley Tribune* early on. "I'm hoping you can tell me if you've seen any of these men."

"You know BJ wouldn't like it," the older of the two said.

"I just want to know if you've seen them picking up girls. And no, I won't even ask for your names. It won't take a minute."

Out of the corner of her eye, Alexa saw that the light over the cross street had turned yellow. Her window of opportunity was shrinking here.

Both had their backs to the street now, so she hastily whipped out the eight photos she'd chosen. Somebody would have to be really close to see that the three women were doing anything but talking.

Neither of the young women could resist letting their gazes drop to the photos Alexa displayed one at a time. Three were faces she'd plucked off the internet, men who weren't even local. This wasn't exactly a blind test, but she tried to convince herself she was coming close.

The older was the first to touch one photograph.

"I think he was seeing a girl who works a few blocks down for a while. I don't know if he does anymore."

Jim Ward.

Alexa nodded. Traffic had started up and, taking a sidelong look, she became aware of a thin, tattooed man getting out of a car parked across the street. BJ, she guessed.

Hurry, hurry.

"Him." The pitifully young blonde poked a photo. "He, um, has a regular." She frowned. "Or he did."

Rick Shanahan.

"I've heard—"

The older girl shushed her and grabbed the pile, flipping quickly through the rest. "Him, too," she said.

Brian Danner. Alexa felt the tiny hairs on the back of her neck prickle.

"He never pays, and BJ doesn't say anything."

Alexa met a blistering stare from the creep across the street and she stepped back. "Thanks, you've been a big help."

She hadn't retreated ten feet when a car pulled to the curb and the blonde sauntered over and bent to talk to the driver through the open window. Now her skirt didn't altogether cover her butt.

If Alexa hadn't been so mad, she might have cried

for a girl who wasn't even old enough to attend a high school prom.

One more block, she decided.

The crossing light changed to green but she looked both ways anyway before stepping into the street. Partway across, some instinct made her turn her head. Her gaze caught on the tall man with tousled nut-brown hair who had just stepped out of a door alcove.

MATTHEW WALKED IN the door to find Alexa standing only a few feet away, arms crossed. "Really?"

He grinned at her. "Surprised you, didn't I?"

She snorted. "I knew you wouldn't be able to resist trailing me. You did stay out of sight better than I expected," she admitted with clear reluctance.

"You didn't know I was there until you saw me," he countered.

"Vince had already spotted you."

"I don't believe you."

She smirked, an expression he found he liked on her face. Her phone appeared in her hand and she opened a string of texts for him.

Looking down, he saw that she had told the truth. It reassured him, in a way, knowing that her driver was that observant.

"You win." He handed her back her phone. "You have any ideas for dinner?"

"I ordered Thai."

He grinned again at the take-it-or-leave-it tone. "Sounds good to me."

Instead of going straight to the kitchen, she led him

to the living room where she plopped down at one end of the sofa. He sat right beside her and wrapped an arm around her. Nuzzling the top of her head, he asked, "Mad at me?"

She sighed. "No. Knowing you were there was… comforting. Every time I crossed a street, I expected a car to come out of nowhere and flatten me."

He shook his head. "Too much foot and vehicular traffic. Nobody would get away with a hit-and-run."

"I guess so."

He let the silence go for the moment, content to be holding her, inhaling the mint smell of her shampoo. Finally, he asked, "Learn anything?"

She tipped her chin up so she could see his face. "Not as much as I'd hoped. One picked out Brian Danner. She told me that he never pays, and her pimp is okay with that. I think a couple of others recognized him, too."

Matthew grimaced. How did these guys live with themselves?

"Only one said she recognized Rick Shanahan, although I could tell the other woman—girl—with her did, too."

"Was that the really young one?"

"You saw?" She shivered. "Can't you arrest a girl like that and get in touch with her family?"

"I tried a few times, early on." He shook his head. "If it's possible to identify family at all, it usually turns out to be toxic. Kids run away for a reason. Sending them back doesn't really work, and they don't tend to be receptive to anything social services offers."

Alexa ducked her head so he couldn't see her face. "I know that. It's just…"

He rubbed his cheek on her head again, until his evening stubble caught strands of her hair. "I know," he murmured.

After a moment, Alexa continued. "She started to say something about Shanahan. That he had a regular. Then she said, 'Or he did.' Past tense. Her partner shut her up."

Because the regular was dead? Body found tossed in a dumpster?

When Alexa asked, Matthew told her about his day. He concluded by saying, "Feel like we're going in circles?"

"Yeah, but we always end up in the same place. Crooked cops."

"I have Danner and Shanahan at the top of my list," Matthew admitted. "I've been able to eliminate a couple of the others for Dwyer's shooting."

She pulled back and raised her eyebrows.

"Mike Swartz and Don Rommel. Swartz's sister got married last weekend. He flew out Thursday to be in Texas for the wedding. Rommel plays bass in what's mostly a garage band. They had a gig Thursday through Sunday night at a local tavern."

She nodded.

"But I keep reminding myself that there could be someone in the background nudging these guys who are running scared because of your investigation."

"And Detective Dwyer's."

"Yeah." He cleared his throat. "Whoever he is, he didn't kid himself that he could steer Art in a new direction or scare him."

Fortunately, security at the hospital was pretty tight in the ICU.

Alexa asked how Art was doing and, for the first time, Matthew was able to sound—and feel—positive. "I'd swear he was trying to respond when I talked to him. He looked grumpy that he couldn't manage it."

She laughed. "I…keep thinking about him."

A moment later, the conversation reverted to where they'd left off, though, when she asked, "Wouldn't anyone expect *you* to take up where Art left off? Or assign another detective to it?"

"Except for me, Art's the most experienced and capable detective in the department. And everyone knows I can't put as much into any investigation because of my administrative responsibilities. Or he could think he's smarter than I am."

Alexa made a rude sound that had him smiling ruefully. Nonetheless, any stir of humor didn't derail him.

"You, though…" He made sure she was paying attention. "They've tried everything, and your response? You're still at it, putting pressure on the city and county, interviewing cops who've been in trouble. You filed suit against the county, and everyone knows what you're really demanding is unlimited access to camera footage and disciplinary records. You're not backing off."

She didn't say a word, but her pupils had dilated. "You think…"

"I do think. He's gotten away with killing one cop. The other is in a coma. He'll think he can kill you, too, and go on his merry way."

Chapter Seventeen

Monday proved to be an astonishingly relaxed day. There wasn't much he could have accomplished if he'd chosen to go in, and he wanted to spend time with Alexa when they weren't discussing killers.

As it was, they slept late and made love a third time upon awakening. She put him to work cleaning house while she did the same, and seemed pleased when he did a few simple repairs that she probably could have accomplished but had put off. The closest they came to talking about the danger to her was when she warned him about the one outing she'd already scheduled for the week: an hour she committed once a month to talking to kids in the alternative school. He thought about trying to dissuade her but didn't want to ruin the mood.

Together, they cooked a fancier than usual dinner that would feed them both for at least three days, then watched TV. He insulted her taste, she insulted his, and they found a middle ground they both enjoyed. As he enjoyed going to bed with her again.

Back in his office Tuesday morning, muscles looser

than they'd been in ten days or more, Matthew got sucked into his job supervising half a dozen current investigations and a request for a warrant that the detective knew was on shaky ground. Matthew sent the detective away to shore up his arguments.

Then, first chance he had, he arranged to meet a dispatcher for coffee. He'd had an idea, which might not turn out to be doable, but he was desperate enough to try anything that might help him be proactive where Alexa's safety was concerned.

Maria Jernberg was the wife of a state trooper, a good friend of Matthew's. Max and he had gone through the police academy together and connected again when Max had been transferred to this region.

Maria was a short, dark-haired, dark-eyed woman who'd worked for Child Protective Services before deciding she needed something less stress-inducing. To everyone's amazement, she apparently missed the word "stress" in the job description and hired on to Dispatch. If Max was to be believed, Maria was thriving.

She jumped up to hug Matthew when he appeared in the break room. She waited until he'd poured himself a cup of coffee and, after a glance around at the half dozen people circling tables, said, "Why don't we sit outside?"

He agreed even though the sky was overcast and the day cool. He let her pick out a picnic table, but before he even swung his leg over the bench, she said, "You want something."

Since they didn't make a habit of taking breaks

together, he guessed he wasn't surprised that she'd read him.

"Yeah, and I don't even know if it's possible."

"What?"

"You need to keep what I'm going to tell you to yourself."

Her eyebrows arched. "Even from Max?"

"Not from Max, but he has to keep his mouth shut, too."

After a frown, she agreed.

He gave her the bare bones, explaining his belief that a cop within the department had killed Alan Sharpe, shot Art Dwyer and was threatening Alexa.

"So what is it you think I can do?" Maria said slowly.

"I'd like to know if either of two men I have my eye on go off the grid. Do they report breaks? Maybe one won't respond to a call because he's not where he's supposed to be? If you find out either has gone AWOL, I want to hear about it."

She thought about his request. "You know I get tied up for twenty minutes or longer when I take a call from someone in real distress."

He set down the disposable coffee cup. "I do."

"That said, I'll try. Can I hint to others on my shift that I've been asked to monitor the activity of a couple of patrol officers?"

He winced. "If this gets out, I could lose my job and so could you."

Her mouth firmed. "Then about all I can do is keep an ear out."

"That's better than nothing."

They talked about other things, but he could tell he'd disturbed her.

On parting, he initiated the hug after he thanked her. "You tell Max to give me a call if he's developed a newfound interest in stripping woodwork."

Maria giggled. "Don't hold your breath. I'm lucky if I can get him to mow the lawn. Now me, I like painting."

"Hey. Why didn't I think to ask sooner?"

"Your loss," she said airily, and they split up.

HE'D BEEN TELLING Alexa more than he should, but he didn't mention that conversation to her. End of the day, he hadn't heard from Maria anyway, which made him realize what a long shot it would be for her to happen to hear another dispatcher trying in vain to reach Shanahan or Danner.

Matthew's tension was winding tighter again, and probably Alexa felt the same, however hard she worked to maintain her "I'm fine. I can handle anything" front. While they ate the dinner of leftovers that evening, they steered clear again of their intersecting investigations or her frustration at being mostly grounded. They watched a couple more episodes from the limited series they'd started last night. He was maybe too distracted to be engaged, but sitting on the couch cuddling Alexa made him happy.

Not so happy that their lovemaking was as tender as he'd intended it to be. Instead, with her willing participation, he took her hard and fast, but even that didn't unwind his gut-deep fear that he'd fail her.

And, damn it, the better the nights with her were, the more Matthew hated leaving her for the day. Yesterday, at least she'd agreed to stay home. When he'd left for work, he'd been glad to see her neighbors hanging over the engine block of a junker in their driveway. He'd waved. They'd looked wary, but he'd believed they'd respond to a screaming woman.

Over breakfast, Alexa had reminded him about her visit to the alternative school.

"I love doing it, and they've been surprisingly engaged. Several of the teachers are doing the same thing—bringing in outsiders to talk about their jobs. Like, a nurse practitioner in a bio class, an IRS agent, believe it or not, in an advanced math class. It's fun." Her expression changed. "I'll bet you'd be welcome—"

Matthew laughed, but actually liked the idea once his focus wasn't so intensely on keeping her safe.

"Can you reschedule?" he asked without a lot of hope.

She just looked at him. "For a week from now? Two weeks? A month?"

Recognizing that he couldn't answer that question, acid ate at his stomach lining. Unless and until there was another attack— Not something he wanted to think about.

"Vince has already agreed to pick me up, wait for me outside and drive me home," she said.

Matthew swore. "Middle of the afternoon?"

"I'm booked for an hour, starting at two thirty. The

school day ends at three thirty, so I won't be alone coming out."

He made a mental note of the time she'd be out, and she promised to text when she made it into the building and then safely home afterward. He was actually a little surprised that a woman as independent as Alexa, as cautious as he sensed she still was with him, was indulging him so readily.

Matthew couldn't let himself think about the longer term, when she *couldn't* do her job without getting out and talking to people.

ALEXA KEPT STEALING looks into the passenger-side mirror. She had a lot of faith in Vince, but couldn't relax the way she would if she were going somewhere with Matthew.

They were moving steadily, and she hadn't seen any particular vehicle making every turn with them. Once, she spotted a squad car stopped at a red light on a cross street as Vince and she went through the intersection, part of a river—well, more like a small stream—of traffic. If the police car turned to follow them, she couldn't see it.

"We're okay," Vince said, making her realize he'd seen her nerves. "In fact, here we are." The turn signal blinked and a familiar Wilden District Alternative School sign appeared on the right. The drive curved through a pretty acre or thereabouts of woods, bright green with the promise of spring that the temperature didn't quite match.

Probably dating to the fifties or sixties, the prosaic, yellow-brick building wasn't huge. Mostly, she could tell which of the couple of dozen cars in the lot belonged to teachers and administrators, and which to students. Vince eased up to the red-painted curb right in front of the double glass doors and braked.

"When you're ready to come out, call me. I'll pull up right here."

She agreed, and he stayed put as she climbed out, closed her door and hustled into the building. Once inside, she stepped to one side and peeked out, watching as the SUV moved to an open slot in the parking lot. She had no idea why she felt so antsy; this was a really unlikely place for someone to launch an attack on her.

Class sizes were nowhere near as big as in the high school. Numbers varied as kids decided to enroll or drop out. The class she'd joined had stayed pretty stable, probably due to the teacher. Alexa really liked Sheila Taft, a plump woman of about her age, possessing what seemed to be unlimited energy and patience both.

The minute Alexa walked into the classroom, a kid named Jeremy Scoleri said, "Hey, you're famous!"

Alexa made a face at him. "And what a pain it is."

She let herself be more up-front with the nine students than she probably should, but she excused herself because part of her role here was to let them into her world. She'd talked before about the ups and downs in journalism, from layoffs to front-page headlines and getting an article picked up by a wire service. Reality was, foreign correspondents risked danger on a daily basis.

She half sat on Sheila's desk at the front of the room.

"Some of what's been happening to me might have been coincidental. I mean stuff happens."

With one voice, they corrected her choice of words, and she laughed. "Remember, growing your vocabulary is important."

"Stuff?" a cheeky girl named Tia said.

"Just pointing out that obscenities are too often used in place of more descriptive words. Don't be lazy, think about stronger words. Used to be, you'd swear and that *was* strong. Now it's commonplace."

She had them rework some sentences until more questions drew her back into her harrowing past few weeks.

"What was it like?" a usually quiet girl asked. "Being kidnapped and tied up and…you know?"

"Terrifying," she said simply. "Afterward…well, the lieutenant who showed up was pretty nice."

"I was in the car once with my dad when we got pulled over and he was arrested," an often sullen boy said. "*Nobody* was *nice*."

"As you know, I had later experiences where that was the case for me, too—" She stopped abruptly. "Hey, you've all been reading the newspaper!"

That caused laughter, some embarrassment, and a warm glow in her chest. They had been. Her visits really were making a difference in their behavior and interests.

MATTHEW STOOD IN his office door and watched Brian Danner walk away down the hall. This interview had been different. Danner was plenty cocky until Matthew had come right out and said harshly, "Your name keeps coming up. You were patrolling in the neighborhood where Detective Art Dwyer was shot. Did you pull that trigger?"

Danner had gaped at him. His mouth opened and closed a few times before he'd managed to talk. "You're nuts! Why are you even asking?"

Matthew let his teeth show. "What about Officer Alan Sharpe. Remember him? Dead because he raised suspicions about his coworkers? Alexa Adams wasn't the only one investigating you and your buddies. Funny that the same gun was used to shoot Sharpe *and* Dwyer—and it was the same one planted under Ms. Adams's car seat. Detective Dwyer had his eye on several of you, too, because he believed one of you didn't just abuse your authority to compel hookers to service you. He knew one of you murdered several of them." Matthew had let contempt infuse his voice. "Does Tansy Elizabeth Gould's name ring any bells, Officer Danner?"

"I— No. Wait. Was she the one found…?"

Had that been shock on his usual smug face?

"Discarded in the dumpster? Carotid artery ripped through by a bullet?"

Danner shot to his feet. "I'm a good cop!"

Matthew sat back in his chair. "Then you might want to tell me where you got that gun. Or which of your friends had it."

Danner had fled. There was no other way to describe it.

And as he now watched the guy's strides get longer and longer until he was almost running, Matthew had to listen to his instincts.

Brian Danner was scum, but he wasn't the killer cop—even though he now had to know who was.

The big question that rose to mind was whether he had enough conscience to come back and answer that last question.

Unsettled, Matthew returned to his desk and picked up his phone. He read again the text from Alexa that had arrived forty minutes ago.

Delivered by Vince, safe. Nobody followed us.

Matthew kept staring at the message. He'd thought he was so smart, scheduling this meeting in the middle of the hour when Alexa would be out and vulnerable. But if Danner *wasn't* guilty of anything but harassment where she was concerned…

He reached for his phone and called Maria Gannon.

"Can you try to locate Rick Shanahan?" he asked, not even attempting to hide his urgency.

"I can try. Did something happen?"

"Not yet. I have a gut feeling. I'm heading out. Call me."

What if he'd misread Danner, who had broken into a run because he was afraid he'd miss Alexa's exit from the school?

Matthew took the stairs two at a time and burst out at the bottom into the lobby. He didn't slow until he hit the parking lot.

MATTHEW MADE HIMSELF stay within the speed limit and resisted the temptation to use lights to clear his way. He'd calmed down a little, helped when he'd seen Danner just sitting in his truck in the parking lot outside the police station.

This was probably stupid. Alexa was still in that classroom along with a bunch of students and a teacher. Neither she nor the hired driver had seen a tail. He could see her rolled eyes when she saw him parked in front of the school.

He didn't even pretend to pray often, but he knew that's what he was doing. His panic made no real sense, but it was real. He kept seeing the moment when Danner had understood he was an accessory to something a whole lot worse than he'd imagined.

Would he call Shanahan? Or conceivably a different dirty cop, the one he knew had supplied that handgun to slip under Alexa's car seat?

Ugly thought.

And if it wasn't Shanahan, Matthew knew he was at an impasse. Brooding, Matthew wondered whether he should have looked harder at John Blykowski, the sheriff's deputy, or Ken Kasperson. Both had apparently had some involvement with prostitutes. Either could conceivably be pulling the strings.

Right now, he had to go with his gut. Either Shanahan or Danner had seemed to be the driver of that last incident leading to the arrest. Alexa might not like having a guard driving home, but she could live with it.

SHEILA BROKE IN. "I'm afraid it's three thirty. You have your assignment for tomorrow. Let's thank Alexa for her time today."

Hoots and applause heightened her good feeling. Kids shoved their textbook and notebooks or tablets in their packs and crowded for the door, sweeping Alexa along with them.

Vince, she thought suddenly, and pulled out her phone.

Other classroom doors hadn't yet opened, so their group was the first to spill out into the hall. When Alexa looked out the glass doors to the parking lot, she saw that Vince was just backing out of the slot toward the back, but he'd be here any minute. She went outside with several of the students clustered around her, Sheila smiling and accompanying them.

Probably making sure no one said anything too outrageous, Alexa in amusement.

Jeremy and another boy asked her what she thought about police officers now, and she stopped where she was, only a few steps from the curb.

"I think most get into it for the right reasons and are trustworthy," she said honestly. "If you looked at people in any profession, I feel sure you'd find bad apples. Keep reading the newspaper and you'll find out about businessmen or women who can't resist the temptation to embezzle more money than they make. Politicians who abuse their position."

"Stinks." Jeremy said.

The SUV had circled the lot and was approaching from her left. She took a step that direction.

Crack.

For one foolish moment, she looked around in bewilderment, not understanding what that sound had been. But then it was followed by more.

Crack, crack, crack.

Gunshots, Alexa realized, shocked as red blossomed on Sheila's chest and she crumpled.

Chapter Eighteen

His phone rang, bouncing on the seat beside him where he'd tossed it. Maria Gannon's number.

"Reinert."

"Shanahan isn't responding on his radio," she said tersely. "He might just be blowing me off, but—"

If she said any more, Matthew didn't hear her. Ending the call, Matthew gain, was unsure whether he'd so much as thanked Maria.

Knowing he had close to half a mile to go, he turned on the flashing lights and accelerated. Once, an idiot driver didn't see him starting into an intersection and came right at him. Matthew gave one blast of the siren and swerved to avoid a collision.

He wasn't far from the turn into the alternative school when his radio crackled to life.

Gunfire at the alternative school. There were people down, the initial callers not sure how many. The school was going into lockdown.

Various units responded, all farther away than Matthew, but he stayed silent, knowing the shooter was listening. Surprise had to be his best tactic.

Driving like a madman now, Matthew still looked for any parked vehicles. A dense stand of deciduous woods separated the road from the school, leaving him blind as he made the turn. Nothing. If Shanahan had parked out here, it wasn't near the entrance. Would he have just driven in? Matthew didn't think so. The guy still thought he could get rid of that journalist and go on in his vicious, corrupt way.

Maybe not Rick Shanahan.

At this moment, it didn't matter who the shooter was. Matthew had to bring him down.

ALEXA SAW THE shock on the face of the boy closest to her. She tackled him and they both went down hard on the concrete. He started to struggle.

"I should be on top. I bet someone is shooting at *you*."

Jeremy. It was Jeremy she'd taken down. She started to lift her head to see what had happened to the others, but the boy rolled her.

"Keep down."

He was trying to protect her with this body. Guilt struck, but that was something she'd have to deal with later. She couldn't live with it if he died in her place. And Sheila…

Jeremy was right. Those shots had been intended for *her*.

Another shot rang out, then another. There was a strange metallic sound, and she knew. Vince had accelerated to use his SUV to try to block those shots. She turned her head, scraping her cheek on the rough surface. The SUV—there it was, a tire up on the curb, the fender connected to a bike rack. She couldn't see Vince at all, and prayed he had thrown himself out of sight. If he was injured…

Sickened, she thought, *I won't make it to him.* But…

"Sheila," she gasped. "I have to—"

Jeremy ignored that. "I dropped my pack. You got your phone?"

Oh. Good thing somebody was using his head. Except people inside would probably already have called 9-1-1 to report gunfire outside. Was anybody in a position to see that one of the teachers had been shot? And what about…oh God, what was his name?

It came to her in a flash. "Brody?" He'd been right here, too.

"He ran back in." The boy sounded as scared as she felt. "I think."

"Are *you* hurt?"

He didn't say anything.

MATTHEW HEARD A blast of gunfire. Had to be from a rifle. Unfortunately, those damn woods provided plenty of cover.

His tires screeched as Matthew rocketed into the parking lot. The rows of cars blocked him from seeing what was directly in front of the school.

Where Alexa might have just come out.

He saw a boy crouched behind one of the nearest cars. The boy's face was blanched white.

Matthew's tires screeched again as he wrenched

the wheel into a sharp left turn that brought him toward the front. He first recognized the SUV hired for Alexa, canted onto the sidewalk, but no sign of the driver. Could Alexa have made it behind the SUV, or even into it to hunker down?

Then he saw the half dozen people out front of the school. All flat on the pavement, unmoving. He didn't let himself try to determine whether they were injured, dead, or just being smart. Glints betrayed the shattered glass of windows and doors at the front of the school. There could be dead or injured inside.

A bullet punched a hole in his windshield and exited at an angle, giving him a good idea where to find the shooter. He had a rifle; he could park and try to take the guy out from a distance. Small movements told him that at least a couple of the people lying in front of the school were alive. He calculated in the way he did when under pressure even as he took in the blood pooling to the side of the woman who lay awkwardly and utterly still. Dark-haired, but... He couldn't be sure, but he didn't think that was Alexa.

He might be able to block them all from the gunfire by pulling up right in front of the cluster, though if he did that, the shooter would escape. And Vince's vehicle was already serving some of the same purpose.

Matthew made a decision to keep going, to accelerate straight for the killer.

Was that Matthew? Alexa couldn't be certain.

"Sheila needs help. We can—" Her voice broke. "We can keep down and wriggle over there."

"That was a cop. He's going to get shot!"

The possibility terrified Alexa. Jeremy was afraid they'd be left completely vulnerable again. *She* was afraid the strong man who'd been asking for her trust, and maybe even more, would die. The thought made her feel as if she was looking into an abyss. There was just…nothing.

Sheila.

"You can stay where you are. Let me—"

"No."

He pushed himself up a few inches. When she squirmed sideways, Jeremy did the same. Alexa was stunned at this boy's courage.

Sheila *looked* dead. Alexa had taken some first-aid classes, but that was all. Pressure on the wound. That was about all she knew.

A fusillade of shots rang out. She tried to flatten herself against the pavement as much as possible, and knew Jeremy was doing the same.

Jeremy jerked, and she cried out. Something stung her cheek. What if this brave boy was killed?

MATTHEW ZIGZAGGED TOWARD the woods, sure now he could see the glint of a scope and the fire of each shot. He hunched as low as he could and still see where he was going. Bullets kept punching holes in the window glass and probably the metal. He'd swear he felt the breeze as one missed his head by a fraction of an inch, but at least now those shots were being aimed at *him*.

That's it, you bastard. I'm coming for you.

It felt as if his swing through the parking lot had

taken forever—minutes, at least, but he knew better. Seconds had a way of stretching during combat.

He wanted to drive straight into the woods and have the satisfaction of seeing the shooter's body slammed by the grille of the SUV, fly into the air, maybe smack the windshield. The trees were too mature, though, so at the back of the lot, he slammed on his brakes, opened his door and threw himself out, crouching behind the door, SIG Sauer in hand.

He took a chance and dropped flat to open fire where leaves fluttered.

Were those running footsteps? Oh yeah. The guy still thought he'd get away.

Glad he was wearing a vest, Matthew launched himself in pursuit.

BLOOD WAS STILL flowing from an awful hole in the teacher's back. That was a good sign, wasn't it? If someone was dead, their heart would quit pumping blood. This was only the exit wound, Alexa reminded herself.

Someone pushed open the glass door.

Alexa yelled, "Stay inside! It's not safe yet!"

The next shots sounded different. A handgun instead of a rifle, maybe? They were a little farther away, too. She risked rising to her knees and tearing off the shirt she wore over a camisole, wadding it up and pressing it to Sheila's back.

"Jeremy?" She looked over her shoulder, realizing for the first time that he, too, had taken a bullet. He was clutching his upper arm, but he wasn't mortally wounded, at least. "I need..."

He pulled his T-shirt over his head and handed it to her. There was blood on the sleeve, which made it less than ideal but still better than nothing. Crouched, like her, he helped her turn Sheila over. The entry wound was higher than Alexa had thought, although it had taken a downward path through her body. Her face was slack; she didn't react at all to being moved. Alexa pressed the cotton fabric to the wound and prayed.

She could hear sirens, several of them. Help was on its way. With her free hand, she fumbled for her phone and pulled it from her pocket.

9-1-1.

"Wilden City Emergency Services," a man's voice said.

"I'm at the alternative school." She heard herself panting. "We have injured people here. I hear sirens. We need ambulances."

"They are en route, ma'am. Are you all right?"

"I'm fine." No, she wasn't fine at all, but he was talking about physical injuries.

"Is the shooter still active?"

"I...don't know. He was a minute ago, but a police unit arrived and I think that officer may be in pursuit." Unless he was dead. From here, she couldn't see the black-and-silver vehicle.

"There's already a law enforcement presence?" He sounded startled.

"Yes. I think he might be Lieutenant Matthew Reinert. Tell anyone coming to watch out for him."

"I will. Please stay on the line—"

She ended the call and dropped her phone.

All she could think was, *Matthew. Please be all right.*

HE CAREENED OFF a tree trunk and spun to one side, not letting himself slow down.

Shaking leaves and the crackle of breaking sticks and branches wasn't twenty feet ahead of him.

"Police!" he yelled. "Stop and lay down your gun."

Pop.

A bullet chipped a nearby tree. At least Shanahan—maybe Shanahan—was firing wildly now, aware he had less than a minute to escape. Matthew had been trying to keep count of shots taken and thought his target must be close to emptying his magazine. Odds were he'd be too shaken to make a change on the run like this. No matter what, his skin must be shredded, as Matthew knew his was, too. Had it occurred to the guy that he couldn't just leap into his vehicle, then drive in as if he, too, were responding to the radio distress call?

Through the foliage, Matthew caught sight of the road and the shine of black metal. If it was Shanahan, had he switched to his own vehicle for this little outing? Damn, Matthew hoped so. That would be the pickup seen in the vicinity of a couple of the murders. However he'd scrubbed out the truck bed, it was hard to eradicate every trace of blood or skin.

The dark shape ahead of him ran right into the truck, bounced off it and circled around the front.

Matthew put everything he had into a last burst of speed, choosing to go around the back. "Drop your weapon!" Matthew ordered one last time.

Shanahan lifted it instead, aiming at point-blank range.

Matthew fired, and kept firing. Shanahan stumbled back into the V formed by the open door, his face changing. Matthew didn't see blood—*vest*, he thought with surprising clarity—and he aimed high, for the throat. He pulled the trigger one last time and saw Shanahan's gun fall to the dirt.

ALEXA SAT ON the pavement as an EMT dabbed at the cut on her cheek with something that stung.

"Are you sure you're not dizzy?" the young woman asked. "You might have hit your head when you went down."

"No, I'm fine," she kept repeating, although that's the last thing she was. She couldn't quit shaking. If only someone would *tell* her what was happening.

Police were everywhere. A while ago, the tense atmosphere and state of readiness had suddenly relaxed, telling her the shooter had either escaped or was down. But which? And what about Matthew? That *had* to have been him, coming to the rescue. Otherwise, he'd have showed up by now. She knew he would have.

Seeing an officer approaching, she said, "Lieutenant Reinert? Do you know—"

His gaze went past her. "He's here."

"Oh, thank God!" She tried to turn, prevented by the EMT.

And there he was, striding toward her, his gaze intense, his stride never deviating. He seemed oblivious to the bustle of activity, just as he had in the alley the first time she'd seen him.

He looked awful, a dark red splotch on his forehead already swelling, scratches dotted with blood everywhere on his face, neck and forearms. But he was alive. Essentially uninjured.

If there hadn't been so many onlookers, she would have burst into tears. As it was, she took a few deep breaths.

He reached her, taking in her incredibly minor wounds from above before crouching in front of her.

"I was so afraid," she whispered.

His gray eyes burned into hers. "You and me both. I couldn't be sure—" He swallowed.

"It was Sheila. The teacher who invited me out here. She got shot instead of me. Have you heard…?"

Two ambulances had screamed away at least fifteen minutes ago. One carrying Sheila. The other, Vince, who, although bleeding, had been able to crawl out to check on Alexa, as well as Jeremy and another student unlucky enough to be grazed by a shot through a window where he'd probably stood to stare out.

"The teacher is alive," Matthew said, his voice gravelly but also…tender. "I'm told they took her right into surgery. Nobody else is hurt badly. It could have been worse."

"If he'd shot me right away, no one else would have been hurt."

Matthew grimaced his empathy. "He must have realized he'd taken down the wrong woman. He'd taken a huge risk, and didn't want to quit without killing you."

Her fault.

No. The man had already been killing women. She couldn't forget that.

As the EMT loaded her supplies in the back of the ambulance and slammed the doors, Matthew said, "I think I used up a couple of my lives."

Alexa's eyes burned but she laughed, too, if with an edge of hysteria. "You and me both. If you'd died—" She couldn't make herself finish.

In that same voice, he laid himself on the line. "I've been falling in love with you. You have to know that."

Damn. Now she *was* crying. "I kept thinking, I never said anything. I'm such a coward."

Not until his expression changed did she realize he'd braced himself. He hadn't been sure of her.

He wrapped her nape with one of his big, strong hands and gave a gentle squeeze. "Not you. You're the bravest woman I've ever known. You...had good reason to distrust me."

"Only at first."

Somebody in a uniform backed into Matthew, momentarily rocking him.

"Who was it?" she asked.

"The man who wanted to kill you? Rick Shanahan." He'd shielded his expression.

"Did you have to kill him?"

"Yes. He made his choice." Matthew shook his head. "He really thought he could pick you off and drive away, nobody the wiser."

Her teeth chattered. "If he'd had even a couple more minutes to get off a few more shots…" She looked at him in bewilderment. "How did you know to come?"

He told her his reasoning then drew her to her feet and pulled her snugly into his arms. "Your friend'll be okay. Have faith."

She searched his eyes. "The boy who got shot in his arm? He put himself in front of me. Jeremy might have saved my life. He's a hero."

"And we'll make damn sure everyone knows he is."

Alexa sighed and stirred against him. "You're not in trouble, are you?"

"For shooting a fellow officer?" His jaw tightened. "No. But a good portion of the Wilden PD is once this all comes out. I predict a bunch of resignations, suspensions and outright firings. As far as I'm concerned, the firing should start at the top."

Alexa rose on tiptoe and kissed him. Then she said, "Leave it to me."

Matthew laughed. "I have full confidence in you."

Amazingly, he always had.

Equally amazingly, her shakes were gone. "So, can we go home?" she asked.

One side of his mouth lifted. "I'm afraid there'll be a few hours of interviews first. After that, the only question is which house will be home?"

This was too soon to go *that* far, and he had to know it. But…she had complete faith the question would come up again, and probably soon. Fortunately, the answer was easy. She'd enjoy working on restoring his historic home. And really, where they lived didn't matter that much, did it?

"But we have to go to the hospital first," she said urgently.

He smiled, kissed her again, and said, "Of course we will."

* * * * *

COMING NEXT MONTH FROM

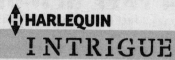

HARLEQUIN
INTRIGUE

#2145 HER BRAND OF JUSTICE
A Colt Brothers Investigation • by B.J. Daniels
Ansley Brookshire's quest to uncover the truth about her adoption leads her to Lonesome, Montana—and into the arms cowboy Buck Crawford. But someone doesn't want the truth to come out...and will do *anything* to halt Ansley and Buck's search. Even kill.

#2146 TRAPPED IN TEXAS
The Cowboys of Cider Creek • by Barb Han
With a deadly stalker closing in, rising country star Raelynn Simmons needs to stay off the stage—and off the grid. Agent Sean Hayes accepts one last mission to keep her safe from danger. But with flying bullets putting them in close proximity, who will keep Sean's heart safe from Raelynn?

#2147 DEAD AGAIN
Defenders of Battle Mountain • by Nichole Severn
Macie Barclay never stopped searching for her best friend's murderer...until a dead body and a new lead reunites her with her ex, Detective Riggs Karig. Riggs knows he and Macie are playing with fire. Especially when she becomes the killer's next target...

#2148 WYOMING MOUNTAIN MURDER
Cowboy State Lawmen • by Juno Rushdan
Charlie Sharp knows how to defend herself. But when a client goes missing—presumed dead—she must rely on Detective Brian Bradshaw to uncover the truth. As they dig for clues and discover more dead bodies, all linked to police corruption, can they learn to trust each other to survive?

#2149 OZARKS DOUBLE HOMICIDE
Arkansas Special Agents • by Maggie Wells
A grisly double homicide threatens Michelle Fraser's yearslong undercover assignment. But the biggest threat to the FBI agent is Lieutenant Ethan Scott. He knows the seemingly innocent attorney is hiding something. But when they untangle a political money laundering conspiracy, how far will he go to keep Michelle's secrets?

#2150 DANGER IN THE NEVADA DESERT
by Denise N. Wheatley
Nevada's numeric serial killer is on a rampage—and his crimes are getting personal. When Sergeant Charlotte Bowman teams up with Detective Miles Love to capture the deranged murderer before another life is lost, they must fight grueling, deadly circumstances...and their undeniable attraction.

Get 4 FREE REWARDS!

We'll send you 2 FREE Books plus 2 FREE Mystery Gifts.

FREE Value Over **$20**

Both the **Harlequin Intrigue®** and **Harlequin® Romantic Suspense** series feature compelling novels filled with heart-racing action-packed romance that will keep you on the edge of your seat.

YES! Please send me 2 FREE novels from the Harlequin Intrigue or Harlequin Romantic Suspense series and my 2 FREE gifts (gifts are worth about $10 retail). After receiving them, if I don't wish to receive any more books, I can return the shipping statement marked "cancel." If I don't cancel, I will receive 6 brand-new Harlequin Intrigue Larger-Print books every month and be billed just $6.49 each in the U.S. or $6.99 each in Canada, a savings of at least 13% off the cover price, or 4 brand-new Harlequin Romantic Suspense books every month and be billed just $5.49 each in the U.S. or $6.24 each in Canada, a savings of at least 12% off the cover price. It's quite a bargain! Shipping and handling is just 50¢ per book in the U.S. and $1.25 per book in Canada.* I understand that accepting the 2 free books and gifts places me under no obligation to buy anything. I can always return a shipment and cancel at any time by calling the number below. The free books and gifts are mine to keep no matter what I decide.

Choose one: ☐ **Harlequin Intrigue Larger-Print** (199/399 HDN GRJK)   ☐ **Harlequin Romantic Suspense** (240/340 HDN GRJK)

Name (please print)

Address   Apt. #

City   State/Province   Zip/Postal Code

Email: Please check this box ☐ if you would like to receive newsletters and promotional emails from Harlequin Enterprises ULC and its affiliates. You can unsubscribe anytime.

> **Mail to the Harlequin Reader Service:**
> **IN U.S.A.:** P.O. Box 1341, Buffalo, NY 14240-8531
> **IN CANADA:** P.O. Box 603, Fort Erie, Ontario L2A 5X3

Want to try 2 free books from another series! Call 1-800-873-8635 or visit www.ReaderService.com.

*Terms and prices subject to change without notice. Prices do not include sales taxes, which will be charged (if applicable) based on your state or country of residence. Canadian residents will be charged applicable taxes. Offer not valid in Quebec. This offer is limited to one order per household. Books received may not be as shown. Not valid for current subscribers to the Harlequin Intrigue or Harlequin Romantic Suspense series. All orders subject to approval. Credit or debit balances in a customer's account(s) may be offset by any other outstanding balance owed by or to the customer. Please allow 4 to 6 weeks for delivery. Offer available while quantities last.

Your Privacy—Your information is being collected by Harlequin Enterprises ULC, operating as Harlequin Reader Service. For a complete summary of the information we collect, how we use this information and to whom it is disclosed, please visit our privacy notice located at corporate.harlequin.com/privacy-notice. From time to time we may also exchange your personal information with reputable third parties. If you wish to opt out of this sharing of your personal information, please visit readerservice.com/consumerchoice or call 1-800-873-8635. **Notice to California Residents**—Under California law, you have specific rights to control and access your data. For more information on these rights and how to exercise them, visit corporate.harlequin.com/california-privacy.

HIHRS22R3

HARLEQUIN
PLUS

Try the best multimedia subscription service for romance readers like you!

Read, Watch and Play.

Experience the easiest way to get the romance content you crave.

Start your **FREE TRIAL** at
<u>www.harlequinplus.com/freetrial</u>.